All Books by Harper Lin

www.HarperLin.com

Croissant Murder

A Patisserie Mystery
Book #5

by Harper Lin

This is a work of fiction. Names, characters, organizations, places, events, and incidents are either products of the author's imagination or are used fictitiously. Some street names and locations in Paris are real, and others are fictitious.

ISBN-13: 978-0992027971

ISBN-10: 0992027977

Contents

Recipes

Chapter 1

"Are they still out there?" Clémence peeked out the window of the Damour *salon de thé*.

"Yup, they are," said Celine, who worked as a hostess. "Still standing around like idiots, waiting for your pretty mug."

Although Clémence's family-owned patisserie chain had the occasional celebrity visitor and it wasn't a surprise to find photographers waiting outside from time to time, Clémence was the target of the paps this time. She wasn't used to this amount of attention from the media. She wasn't a movie star or model or singer. Some still considered her a socialite, but she hardly went out to parties and events anymore. There were four beefy-looking guys chatting and waiting for her by the lamppost.

"They have all day, don't they?" Caroline, the store manager, came by, shaking her head. "Once they get their photo, it's payday. How can they sleep at night, knowing that they're making a living by harassing a young woman that has just been through hell and back?"

Clémence sighed. "Not only that, but our customers just want to enjoy a quiet lunch outside."

It was July, and the weather had been exceptionally amazing in Paris for the past week. No hint of rain clouds and every chance of sunshine. The terrace was full, and everybody looked to be enjoying themselves, except for the looming thugs with cameras, just a few feet away.

"Nonsense." Celine smiled mischievously, her dimples deepening. "They're enjoying the novelty of it all. Half of them are tourists who want a taste of glamor and dining with the elite, and the other half are the elite, who're used to this kind of thing. Don't worry about it."

Clémence was doubtful. She peered out at the paparazzi again, at the nameless and faceless guys in T-shirts and ill-fitting jeans, loitering outside her store for a quick buck.

She'd passed them on the way to work that morning. She was wearing a chic black sun hat and sunglasses, and somehow they *still* managed to recognize her. Compared to the glamorous models, the trophy wives, or the chic mothers in the posh 16th arrondissement, Clémence considered herself quite ordinary. With a black bob haircut and an average, five-foot-four frame, she was only getting attention because of a kidnapping that had made headlines around France. She'd been a victim, along with another heiress, Sophie Seydoux. Sophie, a true socialite and It girl, was used to being in the tabloids and gossip blogs, but Clémence hadn't been part of that world for years.

"They'll give up eventually," she muttered.

Those guys had planted themselves outside of 4 Place du Trocadéro for days now. There had been more of them when the news first broke that Clémence and Sophie Seydoux had been kidnapped and held for ransom. That was over a week ago. Both girls had been bombarded with interviews to talk about their traumatic experiences. Sophie already had a talent agent to deal with the calls and interview requests, but Clémence had no one.

She first saw herself splashed on the cover of tabloids wearing that infamous lavender Marcus Savin dress, which was now causing some sort of fashion frenzy and raised the talented designer's profile even more. Tabloid magazines wrote features about her, and they even dug up old photos of her from other events, dating back to when she was eighteen. They dissected her street fashion, her relationship with her boyfriend Arthur, and churned out sensationalistic pieces on the kidnapping.

The truth was, Sophie was the one who had suffered the most. She'd been missing for six days.

By the time she was found, she'd smelled since she hadn't showered at all, and she'd lost six pounds because they barely fed her. She'd been handcuffed to a chair during the day. At night, they locked her in a bare room with only a pillow and a blanket; she had to sleep on the floor. Sophie was the one who'd gone through the real horror.

Clémence had only been held for a few hours. She didn't deserve the media attention; they were spinning it to say she was some sort of hero. She'd tried to set the record straight, but the journalists didn't listen. They preferred the original angle; they needed a hero and a bad guy, and she had to play the role of the good guy in all of this in order for the stories to sell.

It wasn't a bad position to be in, except that all the attention was causing plenty of stress. Paris could be stressful enough to live in to begin with, especially during the summer, with its narrow and crowded streets, flocks of tourists, and sniffy locals offended by anything and everything. What she enjoyed about the city—the beauty, the architecture, the river, the bridges, the parks and the walks—were now tainted by the paranoia of being followed by a bunch of guys with cameras. Take away the cameras, and what did she have? A bunch of guys following her around. She couldn't even walk into her own store without lights blinding her. She also wondered whether customers were really staring at her and talking about her under their breaths, or if she was just imagining things.

But she tried to be positive. For the past few days, she'd had to remind herself that she was lucky. Lucky that she wasn't still being held—or possibly killed, as that was what the kidnappers had planned to do before the police came to the rescue. Better that she was suffering through a media storm than having her parents shell out millions and still end up with a dead daughter.

No matter. It was all behind her, and this would all blow over soon enough, too. No more murders, no more kidnappings, no more tabloids and paparazzi and journalists harassing her for interviews. Clémence Damour would return to being a baker in the family's flagship patisserie and moonlighting as a budding painter. She would return to basking in the freshness of her new romance with her boyfriend Arthur—who happened to be rounding the corner and passing the paparazzi.

The paps recognized Arthur, too—he'd been photographed next to her at the police station when she was wearing that gorgeous lavender Savin dress.

The photographers called his name and began snapping away, but Arthur had his Persol sunglasses on and maintained a neutral expression. He wore a white V-neck T-shirt and his favorite dark-blue jeans. His chestnut-brown hair was overgrown, since he'd been through a lot, too, and hadn't had the chance to go to the barber. Even as one guy filmed him and bombarded him with questions, Arthur kept cool and maintained his normal pace.

It was only after he pushed through Damour's front door that he muttered expletives. The paps stayed outside, knowing that they didn't have the rights to film or photograph them inside. If they did, the police would be called.

"*Bonjour, chéri.*" Clémence kissed him hello. "*Ça va?* Are you okay?"

"Yeah. I'm not bothered by a bunch of low-class leeches." He took a few deep breaths. "Ready to go?"

They had plans to lunch at La Coquette, which was only a few doors down, but Clémence was hesitant about going outside again.

"If only there were a back door we could escape through," she said.

"Don't let those guys get to you," he said. "They'll get tired of coming around here sooner or later and move on to the next story of the week. Don't they usually get bored and leave later in the afternoon?"

"Yes, so can't I hide until then?"

"Come on. Just act like they don't exist. You can't put your life on hold because of some vultures."

"I know, I know...but maybe we can just eat here."

Arthur gave her a look, one that said that she was being a wuss.

"Oh, all right," she said. "Let me get my sunglasses, at least."

When she reemerged from the back room, she and Arthur both put on their sunglasses. They were cool enough to take on the world, or at least appear to. Clémence had worn all black for the day, to stay incognito. She looked like a French spy.

However, before they could go out into the chaotic crowd, she could've sworn she saw a couple of the customers snap photos of her from the salon de thé.

She took a deep breath before she pushed the door open.

"Clémence! Clémence! Was the kidnapper really your ex-boyfriend?"

"Is Sophie really in therapy for trauma?"

"What exactly did they do to you when you were held hostage?"

"Are you going on La Grand Journal this week?"

"Why aren't you doing interviews? Don't you want to tell the world your story?"

Clémence now understood why celebrities had to wear sunglasses all the time. It was easier to look unfazed and dignified. She didn't want to talk about the kidnapping because it was over. Her captors had been caught. One was even dead. Sophie had become a recluse, and Clémence didn't blame her. They both wanted to forget the whole thing. Why drag it into a media circus when justice had already been served?

Arthur squeezed her hand tighter, communicating that he had her back. He was even more private than she was, but lately he'd been dragged into the tabloids and the blogs with her. They'd even dug up information on his private life, only the basic facts, even though there was nothing juicy—how he was from a prominent family, how he had gone to the best schools, and how he was currently doing a PhD in macroeconomics at Paris Dauphine University. Because he was tall with broad shoulders and had a killer bone structure, he was being profiled in the media as a former playboy turned devoted boyfriend. Their love story was tabloid fodder. It was embarrassing for both of them, especially because their relationship was so new that their parents had only found out about it recently.

At La Coquette, Arthur requested a table in the very back corner, away from any windows.

"I got a phone call today from a publisher," he said, when they were seated. "*Editions Laberg*. The guy said they left a message with you, but you'd never called back. They wanted me to pass on the message."

"What's it about?" Clémence asked. "I have about a hundred messages from numbers I don't recognize. I'm seriously thinking of changing my phone number."

"They want to give you a book deal for a memoir."

"A memoir? About the kidnapping?"

"Yes. And about your patisserie, your family, the Seydoux girls, everything."

"I'm surprised they haven't found out that I was linked to the other murder cases," she said.

"The police probably don't want that stuff to get out," he said, chuckling a little. "That'll cast them in a bad light. Imagine if the public found out that a baker has been solving the murder cases all along, while the police can't seem to put two and two together."

Clémence couldn't help laughing too, thinking of the volatile Inspector Cyril St. Clair. "It's not as if it's not common knowledge already how incompetent the inspectors are in this city. So what did you tell the publisher?"

"That you're probably not interested, but that I'd pass the request on to you anyway. You're not, right?"

"No way. I bet they offered the same deal to Sophie Seydoux. I wish they'd be more sensitive. It's barely been a week since she was released."

Arthur snorted. "Please, it's the media. When did they ever go through sensitivity training?"

Clémence looked up at Arthur from her menu. She'd fallen in love with him earlier that summer. Sure, he had his flaws, but it didn't matter. She was smitten, which made it all the more painful for her that she had to break some rather sensitive news of her own.

"So, uh..." She cleared her throat. "I have something to tell you."

Arthur frowned at the change in her tone. "What is it?"

"I took an unexpected call this morning, too. My ex-boyfriend Mathieu called me."

Chapter 2

That very morning, Clémence had woken up with a dry mouth and a feeling of dread. Arthur was an early riser, and he'd emerged clean and dressed from the bathroom before she was even fully conscious. He kissed her good-bye because he had to go in to J&D Consulting Agency, where he worked part time.

Alone in the apartment with Miffy, her white Highland terrier, Clémence played with her a bit, then poured dog food into her bowl. Aside from Arthur, Miffy was her rock. While Clémence was still reeling from the aftermath of a kidnapping, Miffy cheered up with her mere presence.

Miffy was her parents' dog. Clémence was house-sitting and dog-sitting for them while they were in Asia until at least October, splitting their time between Tokyo and Hong Kong to oversee the new Damour patisseries that had just opened in those two cities.

When her parents had found out about the kidnapping, they'd called Clémence and told her they were boarding the next flight back. She had to spend over an hour on the phone to convince them that everything was under control. She had to admit to them that Arthur had moved in with her so they wouldn't worry about her living alone. She'd also installed a more advanced security system, which she turned on with a remote when she went to sleep.

It had been a stressful week, indeed. Every time she thought she had her life together, something happened. Everything that had happened during the past few months had instilled more fear. She was afraid of losing everything that mattered to her. Being so close to death could do that to a girl. That, and seeing countless dead bodies.

She also questioned who she could trust. *How well could you know a person?* The most recent example of betrayal was between Sophie and Juan. And what about Rose and Pierre? All betrayals. Maybe the girls could have read the signs and prevented these tragedies from happening.

Her relationship with Arthur was new, but it might not last. Arthur could get tired of her. It had happened before, with Mathieu. If there was one thing she learned from her short career as an amateur sleuth, it was this: trust no one.

The division between the good guys and bad guys was not clear cut; the world wasn't so black and white. The reasons some people killed and some people died weren't a matter of evil people versus victims. There was always the possibility that somebody would betray her. She could succumb to ego and selfish desires herself and betray somebody she cared about.

Adding to the stress was the matter of her birthday. It was almost three weeks away. She was turning twenty-nine this year. It wasn't too bad, she kept telling herself. She'd accomplished quite a bit and she lived a fruitful life—a good job, great friends, travels around the world behind her, and now a hot new boyfriend. She didn't know why she was feeling uneasy.

Birthdays always did that to her. It sharpened the things that were usually out of focus. It happened every year, this familiar dread and the need to get incredibly drunk. She hope it didn't mean anything—age was just a number, after all. But she didn't quite believe it.

All her life, she'd aspired to be a painter. She always told herself that it didn't matter whether she made it as an artist, but the truth was that she was nearly thirty, and she'd never done anything to realize her dreams. All she had accomplished in her life, really, was to work in a fun, cushy job at her parents' patisserie and get lucky with a few murder cases.

All these negative thoughts were weighing her down. It was one of those days when she questioned everything. She thought too much, and it gave her a headache.

She sighed, and Miffy looked up at her with her curious, dark eyes as if to ask what was the matter.

"It's nothing." Clémence felt the need to shrug it off and maintain a strong front, even to her family's dog. "It'll pass. Don't worry about me."

Miffy made a high-pitched squeal, and her lips upturned, as if she wanted to smile and cheer her up. Clémence smiled back. She got down on the floor and patted Miffy's head.

As her mood lifted, her cell phone rang. Clémence had been her screening calls all week, only answering when she recognized the number. The previous night, she'd cleared over fifty messages on her voicemail without listening to most of them.

He's a cheater and a LIAR!!! flashed on her smartphone screen. Clémence's heart sank. She knew who it was.

She'd changed her ex-boyfriend Mathieu's name on the contact list to *He's a cheater and a LIAR!!!* to prevent herself from drunk-texting him when she was feeling vulnerable. She should've deleted his number altogether, and she wondered why she didn't. Maybe she'd expected him to call one day. And today was that day.

"*Allô?*" she answered tentatively.

"Clémence Damour," Mathieu's deep, confident voice boomed from the other end. "C'est Mathieu. It's been a while. *Ça va?*"

"*Oui, ça va? Et vous?*"

"*Vous?*" Mathieu was quick to catch the formal way she addressed him. "I thought we would be beyond the formalities by now."

"Right." Clémence let out a forced laugh, mainly to calm her own nerves. "So...what's up?"

She cringed at how uptight she sounded. Why couldn't she be cool and suave like he was?

"First of all, I wanted to see how you were doing," he said, concern in his voice. Of course he knew she'd been kidnapped, and he just wanted to reach out to her. "I heard you've been through a lot lately. How is everything?"

"I'm alive," she said, forcing another laugh. "Everything's okay."

"I wanted to check up on you, see how you're doing. You're okay with that, right?"

"Of course. I appreciate it. How are you?"

"Oh, the same old. I'm set up here in Les Lilas. Finally have a proper space to work on large canvasses."

"Wow, that's great."

"I just moved in three months ago, and I share a space with someone. He's not an artist, but wants to learn, so it's a good trade-off."

Clémence wondered where Sarah fit into the picture. She was the gorgeous nude model he'd dumped her for, and they had been living together, the last she heard. Not that she cared much anymore.

"Sounds amazing," she said.

"Listen, I was wondering if you wanted to catch up sometime. Have a coffee."

"Catch up? Oh, I don't know—"

"I feel like there was never closure between us. I know you have a boyfriend now. It's all over the tabloids. But since we were a big part of each other's lives, it can't hurt to have a friendly chat, right?"

"I suppose it would be okay," Clémence said slowly.

"Great! And something strange had happened to me recently that I thought you'd find interesting."

"Strange? How do you mean?"

"Oh, it's a long story. I'll tell you later. Is tomorrow afternoon all right? Say, four o'clock at Café Dennis?"

It was the café they used to go to all the time when they went to art school together. She hadn't set foot in that café for years.

"Okay. Sure," she replied.

After telling him about Mathieu's call, Clémence tried to gauge Arthur's reaction. Sometimes the man was unreadable. His expression remained stoic, unchanged, but she knew him well enough to sense that he was annoyed. His eyes betrayed more than he'd like. He was like a poker player who needed sunglasses to guard his hand.

"Are you cool with that?" she asked.

"Is this the boyfriend who cheated on you?"

She nodded. "Yup. The very same."

Arthur knew what had happened between her and Mathieu. She'd gone to art school with Mathieu and had the biggest crush on him. All the girls did. When they graduated, Mathieu finally noticed her, and they began going out. They even lived together for a few years until he dumped her for one of his nude models, as cliché as that sounded.

"Do you really want to meet him, or are you just trying to be nice?" Arthur asked calmly.

"I think he mainly wants to apologize. And I'd be open to hearing it. But only if you aren't uncomfortable with the idea."

He shrugged. "I'm okay with it. Go ahead."

"Besides," she added quickly. "He said there's something strange he wants to tell me, but he said it was a long story."

"I guess he knows you. Knows that you like a bit of mystery and intrigue."

"I just want to be clear that I have no remaining feelings for Mathieu. What he did to me was unforgivable, and I've moved on, with you. Sometimes I do feel a little bitterness about what he did. Okay, a lot of bitterness. I want to get past it—get some closure, you know. Not be friends exactly, but friendly. You know you're completely over somebody if you talk to them and know that they have no effect on you whatsoever."

Arthur nodded again, very careful to conceal his feelings. The fact that he couldn't just tell her how he really felt annoyed her. They used to be more open before they got together, and now they were always fighting and butting heads.

"Okay," he replied. "Tell me how it goes." No hint of annoyance in his voice. *Could he really be this cool with it?*

She tried to consider whether she'd be okay if it were his ex wanting to have coffee with him. No, she wouldn't be cool at all. But she'd act the same, to avoid appearing jealous.

She couldn't help feeling guilty. She looked up, and Arthur was smiling at her, to her surprise. She loved the way his eyes crinkled when he did. Even though she knew a few customers were probably watching, she stood up and leaned over the table to kiss him.

"*Je t'aime beaucoup. Tu sais?*" she muttered. *I love you. You know that?*

This man was still looking at her with adoration despite the fact that she was going to meet her ex-boyfriend tomorrow afternoon for coffee. And she was grateful to him.

Still, she had this nagging feeling. Speaking to Mathieu had made her feel uneasy. Meeting him felt wrong. Could she honestly say that she had no feelings for him?

Chapter 3

"**I**'m starting to think Sebastien's gay," Berenice Soulier said matter-of-factly.

On Clémence's balcony, Berenice took a drag of her cigarette. She and Ben, who lived on the top floor of Clémence's building, were over at her apartment for lunch. With the sunny weather streak they'd been having lately, Clémence thought it would be nice to make the most of the sunshine with her friends.

Ever since Ben and Berenice started dating a few months ago, they'd been inseparable. Ben was a writer from England, and Berenice worked alongside Sebastien Soulier, her brother, as a baker at Damour.

The fact that "B Squared," as Clémence referred to Ben and Berenice now, got together because Clémence introduced them on a night out had given her hope at first that she had the talent to be a matchmaker. But it was a hit-or-miss venture. Celine had gone out with Sam, Ben's friend, and they had been hot and heavy for a month, until Sam cooled off and began looking for greener pastures. Celine had moved on as well with an indie rocker.

"He's not gay," Clémence protested. "Why do you think that?"

"It's obvious," she said. "Why didn't I come to this conclusion earlier? This explains all the secrecy, doesn't it? Sebastien even missed family dinner a couple of weeks ago for the Paris Gay Pride parade. He claims he went to support his friend Ted."

"That doesn't mean anything," Clémence said. "There are lots of straight people at that event."

Sebastien was straight as far as Clémence knew. He was going out with a girl named Maya. He just didn't want his sister and his family to know. Even Clémence wasn't supposed to know, but she had run into him at the Spinoza Atelier, where she took art classes on Tuesdays and Thursdays, and discovered that he was taking adult ballet classes with Maya.

"To think," Berenice continued, "my own brother, and I missed all the signs. He's always been neat, and a very good dresser. He knows how to dance and enjoys movie musicals. He cooks and bakes, lives by himself, and hardly takes an interest in girls when we go out, even when they're hitting on *him*. Let's face it: he's as gay as a rainbow."

Clémence tried to suppress her laughter. "Don't jump to conclusions."

"The thing with French men is that they all seem gay," Ben contributed. "They're all dressed really well, so it's hard to tell. Why don't you just ask him?"

"I don't want to be insensitive," Berenice said dramatically. "What if he's embarrassed about it? It's a big event in someone's life, coming out of the closet."

"Maybe Ben's just a quiet, secretive guy," Ben said. "It doesn't necessarily mean he's gay. When's his birthday?"

"October thirtieth. Why?" Berenice asked.

"Oh, he's a Scorpio." Ben nodded knowingly and took a sip of his beer.

"What about it?" Clémence asked.

"Scorpios are known for their secrecy. They're all about control, so they like to hold information back from others so they can hold all the cards. They're quite intense, but they're ambitious and successful. Sounds like Sebastien."

Berenice regarded Ben with surprise. "How do you know so much about astrology?"

"My mother," he said. "She's actually a professional astrologer."

"No way," Clémence exclaimed. "That's cool. I'm a Cancer. What am I like?"

"Cancer is a water sign. You're sensitive, emotional, intuitive, and it's hard for you to trust, but you're loyal and honest with the people you do."

Clémence nodded. "Yeah. That sounds about right."

"You should ask my mom to do a full chart sometime, although she's booked until the end of August."

"She's that good?" Berenice sounded impressed.

"Yup. She even has quite a few celebrity clients. In fact, she was the one who told me to come to Paris. Said the energy was a bit easier for me here, and that I would get more inspiration."

"Did it turn out to be true?" Clémence asked.

"Sure. Especially with all the murders. I can write a series of crime novels based on all the things you've experienced, Clémence."

"That's true." Clémence chuckled. "I'm glad the media hadn't made the connection between Damour desserts and the murders. Sometimes I wonder if that inspector is right. Are our products cursed?"

"No," Ben said. "Damour macarons and pastries are ubiquitous. Go into any Parisian's home, and there's a fifty-fifty chance that they'll have something from Damour."

"Yeah, you can't help it if those poor murder victims happen to love our baked goods," Berenice added.

"Speaking of Cancer, that's this month. Is your birthday soon?" Ben asked.

"Oh." Clémence took a sip from her glass of white wine. "Right. Yeah. It's coming up at the end of the month."

"That's soon, then," Berenice said. "I can't believe I didn't know! We have to do something."

"Nah." She shook her head. "Twenty-nine isn't a big deal. Maybe I'll skip it altogether."

"Come on. Let's have dinner or something, at least. Better yet, let's throw a huge party."

"No. It's been a crazy year so far. I think I'll skip it. Maybe we'll have a drink, but that's it. As for a bash, I don't need the media attention right now."

"I bet people are coming out of the woodwork to talk to you now that you're more famous, huh?" Ben asked.

"Well..." Clémence told them about her ex calling her out of the blue. She'd been dying to tell someone, and she felt that Ben and Berenice would understand. "I feel weird about seeing him, but I couldn't say no. He sounded casual and genuinely nice."

"But you still hate him, don't you?" Berenice watched her closely. They'd been friends for five years, ever since Berenice started working at the patisserie, and she knew how hurt Clémence had been when Mathieu dumped her. The breakup was the main reason Clémence had taken off for two years to travel around the world.

"No, I don't hate him. I can't say I forgive him one hundred percent, but I want to get past it."

"You will," said Ben, who was more cool about things. "There's no harm. You've both moved on. Why not have a friendly drink?"

"When are you going?" asked Berenice.

"Actually, this afternoon. We're supposed to meet at Café Dennis."

"Are you nervous?"

Clémence shrugged. "I'm fine."

But she wasn't—not completely. If she had to admit it to herself, she was a teensy bit nervous.

At the last minute, she asked Mathieu to come to Damour instead. She had good reasons for the change in plans. First, the paparazzi could spring up anywhere, and she didn't want pictures of her with Mathieu on a café terrace to show up on the Internet or the tabloids. It might upset Arthur, even though he knew about their rendezvous already. Secondly, Mathieu was the one who wanted to talk to her. He should come to her.

He obliged willingly, and Clémence reserved her corner table in the *salon de thé*. At Damour, she would be in control. She had her friends around for moral support, and they would be seated away from the windows and the photographers.

At four p.m. on the dot, Mathieu entered, which surprised her because punctuality wasn't his strong suit. He had shaggy, dirty blond hair, light blue eyes, and white teeth that were a bit too big for his mouth. He wasn't as tall or classically handsome as Arthur, but he had a certain bohemian charm.

She wondered if Ben, being a writer, would get along with him. Mathieu was just as talented and creative. The last she checked, the art world was still in love with him.

Mathieu smiled broadly at her as he approached. Clémence stood up to greet him. Although she told herself that she couldn't care less, she had been extra careful with her appearance that morning. She used a straightening iron on her bob and wore a little more makeup than she was used to on a weekday. Just before their meeting, she'd put on more lipgloss, another layer of mascara and reapplied pink blush for a natural glow. She was seeing an ex-boyfriend, after all. She couldn't not look good.

He was wearing ripped, faded blue jeans, a gray T-shirt, a navy hoodie, and Bensimon sneakers. Even though he was the same age as Clémence, he still looked and dressed the same that he had in his early twenties. He'd always dressed super casually. Somehow he made the look work, even in Paris, when everyone was classically dressed. Only Mathieu could make a hoodie look stylish on his skinny frame. Clémence would say that his style was normcore before normcore became a thing.

She had to admit that she still found him attractive. He'd always been inexplicably appealing to girls, since his features were average. The thing about Mathieu was that he didn't care too much about what people thought of him. It was why everyone else was so in awe of him. He was an individual.

She wished she didn't care about what people thought of her either. Especially now, with the media breathing down her neck. If only she could tell them what was on her mind without bracing for a backlash.

"You look amazing," he remarked as he sat down across from her.

"*Merci.*"

Ana, one of the waitresses, came by to take their orders.

"What will you be having?" she said, giving Clémence a knowing look.

"I'll just take a chocolate milkshake," Clémence replied. Damour made a killer hot chocolate, all thick and creamy, like a rich chocolate bar melted down. But since it was summertime, she took the cold version of their famous drink.

"A *café crème* with a croissant, *s'il vous plait*," Mathieu turned back to her, looking at her almost shyly. "You know, I couldn't go into Damour for a year after we broke up."

"*Pourquoi?*" Clémence asked. *Why?*

"Well, what else? Guilt. I was such an ass. We were living together, and we were in love. I don't know why I had to go and...betray you like that."

I don't know either, Clémence wanted to say, but she bit her tongue, only nodding, listening.

"So I guess what I'm trying to say is, I'm really sorry. Can you forgive me?"

Clémence leaned back in her chair, examining him. He looked at her expectantly, eyes wide like a vulnerable puppy.

Had she forgiven him, truly? She'd tried to distract herself from the bitterness for the past two years, but seeing him now in the flesh, she didn't feel the resentment any longer.

He wasn't the best-looking guy, the most well dressed, or the one with the status or wealth, but he was the coolest. Her twenties were marked by her relationship with Mathieu. They were in a relationship for three years, but they had known each other for much longer, ever since they started university. That was a decade ago, Clémence realized.

"Of course I forgive you," Clémence said.

Mathieu looked relieved.

Their drinks came, along with Mathieu's croissant on a porcelain plate.

"I did ultimately go back and buy Damour croissants once in a while," Mathieu said. "When I used to live around the Latin Quarter with Sarah, I would pass by the Damour in the sixth with longing, and one day I finally snapped and bought one."

Sarah was a beautiful girl with long reddish brown hair and smooth white skin, with globes for breasts and a big ass—he simply couldn't resist the temptation at the time. But Clémence didn't cringe at the sound of her name like she thought she would. *Sarah.* It was okay. She hoped they were happy.

"But now you guys are living in Les Lilas?"

"Well, I do. Sarah and I are no longer together."

"Oh. That's too bad." She didn't know what else to say. There was nothing else to say. She was afraid that showing too much concern would seem insincere.

He bit into the croissant and a look of joy spread over his face. "This croissant is orgasmic. I can't get over it. How do you guys do it?"

She shrugged. "Every baker back there is world class."

"Including you," he said.

"I'm all right."

"You were always modest." He smiled at her. Clémence was relieved, glad to have this friendly feeling between them. "How are you doing anyway? Are you still painting?"

"I was painting again," Clémence said. "Starting to, except I've been, well, busy lately."

It dawned on Mathieu. "Oh. The kidnapping. I'm such an idiot. Of course. Here I am going on about myself. What happened? Are you okay?"

Clémence gave him the basic facts, things he had probably read in the news. Mathieu nodded, hanging on her every word, finding every detail fascinating. She supposed it was, as horrifying as the experience had been.

"Anyway," she said. "It's really not a big deal. Sophie's the one who really suffered through the whole ordeal."

"Is she okay? I heard she's in therapy."

"She's getting help," Clémence said vaguely, not wanting to betray Sophie's confidence. "Let's not talk about that anymore. What have you been doing these days, career-wise?"

"Oh." He frowned. "You haven't heard about my shows?"

"No. I've been out of the country for two years, traveling around."

"Oh. Right. I heard about that through the grapevine. Did you come back only recently?"

"Yes, in the spring. When we broke up, I deleted you from Facebook and all that."

"Ouch. I guess I deserved that. I wouldn't want to follow me either, if I were you."

"So what have you been up to? Last I heard, you were doing well with your own show."

"Right," he said. "That show got good reviews. Sold some paintings, and I was doing well there."

"Making a name for yourself, right? Do you still go out a lot?"

She was referring to the parties they had gone to together, back when she could be considered a proper socialite. She had been much more active on the social scene back then, and she'd introduced him to all sorts of people who eventually led to him getting his first exhibition at a small gallery.

"I tried to, but not recently. When I was with Sarah—well, she wasn't that into it."

"Oh. Too bad. Hey, so what's this strange thing that you wanted to tell me?"

"Oh." Mathieu chuckled. "Well, I thought you'd get a kick out of this. I think my place in Les Lilas is haunted. I was thinking of calling you when I made the discovery. Funny enough, you started appearing in the news, and I knew I had to get in touch with you."

Clémence leaned in, eyes wide. "What do you mean your house is haunted?"

"Yeah. There's a ghost in my house for sure. And I have proof."

Chapter 4

"What proof?" Clémence exclaimed. "Tell me!"

Mathieu chuckled. "I knew you'd be into this. It's really bizarre. I mean, I really hope it's not true, but evidence points to the contrary."

"What kind of evidence?"

"Well, I painted the walls in my room recently, but before the paint dried, a handprint appeared. It's still there."

Clémence's mouth hung open. "A handprint? And it's not yours? What if it was your roommate's?"

"I doubt it," he said. "Gille's in London for the month, and no one's been over this week, when the handprint appeared. It can't be either of us, because you know what the creepy thing is?"

"What?"

"It's a tiny handprint, a small child's."

"Your place is being haunted by a child?"

"Possibly. Which is why I'm not that creeped out. But I still want to know how to get rid of this ghost."

"Can I see it?" Clémence asked.

"See the handprint? Sure."

He finished the rest of his *café crème* and reached for his wallet.

Clémence laughed. "Come on. Have you forgotten already? It's my café. Your money's no good here."

"Thanks," he said. "But I'm going to buy a few more of your croissants to take home. So you want to come over now? If you have the time, that is."

"I can, but can I meet you there?"

"Oh, you don't want to take the Métro together?"

"It's best if we don't get photographed together," Clémence said.

"Right." Mathieu nodded, grimacing. "Those guys outside. That's for you?"

"Yup. I'm trying, as much as possible, to avoid being written about. If they see how boring I am, they'll leave me alone."

"I see. Sorry they're hounding you."

"Ah, it's all right. Actually I just don't want there to be any crazy rumors. If I'm seen leaving with an ex-boyfriend, they're bound to make up stories. Not that I care, but I just want to protect my boyfriend."

"Right. I've seen a profile of you guys in the papers. You're quite serious, then."

"Yes." Clémence smiled. "Everything's going well. We're living together."

"I'm happy for you."

Did Clémence detect a hint of jealousy in his voice?

While Mathieu headed to the Métro station, Clémence decided to pick up some white sage. Although she'd never seen a ghost, she was a believer. She knew that one of the ways to get rid of negative energies in a house was by burning white sage. There was a shop in Belleville that sold it, and she quickly picked some up, then jumped back in her cab to head to the address Mathieu had given her.

In Les Lilas, the cab stopped in front of a two-story house with its façade. painted a burnt yellow. Mathieu was already waiting for her outside the gate. He greeted her, once again, with a kiss on each cheek, even though it was unnecessary, as they'd seen each other half an hour earlier.

He pushed open the gate, and she followed him, walking past the well-groomed front yard. The middle-class neighborhood was quiet and residential. A dog barked in the distance, and there were no other people in sight. *At least there aren't any paparazzi around*, Clémence thought.

"You live in this house?" Clémence asked. "It's not divided into apartments?"

He let her into the foyer, where there was a massive staircase to the left. To her surprise, the decor inside was white and minimalist. There was nothing on the walls, except a television mounted on one in the living room, where there was also a fireplace. An African sculpture was on the mantelpiece, as well as a small photograph of a bespectacled man she assumed was the roommate, stroking a tiger. It faced cream white couches and a coffee table made from blue and gray stained glass, the only colorful thing in the room.

"Nope. It's really Gille's house, and I'm renting a room from him."

"Wow," she exclaimed. "It's huge. You can fit six more people in here."

She wasn't exaggerating. It was rare to find big living spaces in Paris. Although the house was not exactly in central Paris, she was still impressed. She remembered the cramped apartment she had shared with Mathieu when they were both fresh graduates. They both paid an arm and a leg for a tiny studio where there was no privacy between them.

"It's great, huh? I'll give you a tour."

They passed the sleek kitchen with modern appliances and counter tops that were bare, except for the espresso machine and two familiar lavender bags with gold Damour logos embossed on them—after their meeting earlier, Mathieu had bought two more croissants to bring home.

He showed her a huge open space in the back of the house, adjacent to the living room, where a couple of easels had been set up. There were canvases of all different sizes leaning against the walls. Floor-to-ceiling glass windows allowed plenty of light in and had an expansive view of the backyard.

"And this is our workspace," Mathieu said. "Where the real magic happens."

"I can see why you moved out here," she said. She painted on her tiny balcony, which was enough for her for now, but it wouldn't be if she ever wanted to work on larger canvases, as Mathieu was doing.

She examined the two art pieces he was working on. One was on an easel and another was drying against the wall. She felt a tinge of jealousy.

"This is great." She pointed to the six-foot canvas that was drying. It had a Modigliani influence with its pastel-splattered background, but the pale figure of a woman was battered with shades of dark grays and blues. Her gray eyes were sad, and her thin lips were downturned. There was an alien quality about her head, and her body was tiny in proportion to it.

"It's part of my new portrait series," he explained, "except these people aren't real. I'm painting them from my head."

He'd always paid great attention to detail, but his style was becoming more distinct. Looking at the sophistication of his work, she felt that her own work was like child's play in comparison. She was painting desserts, for crying out loud.

It was typical of her to feel insecure about her own talents whenever she compared her work to Mathieu's. He had always been the great talent, and she the hack. He inspired her while making her feel terrible about herself at the same time.

He was the kind of artist who could simply close his eyes and produce a masterpiece. Clémence did not possess that raw talent. She was a worker bee. It took her weeks, or even months, to produce something to match Mathieu's caliber, and even then she didn't think it was good enough. What made a piece of art special was such a mystery—what gave it a special edge over the other paintings? Whatever that required, Mathieu had *it* in droves.

The other piece was of a black man with dread-locks down to his chin. Lines creased under his eyes, and there was blood splattered on his cheeks. It seemed to be the theme so far: sullen, withdrawn characters with bloody, battered bodies, calmly placed in front of a pastel backdrop.

Mathieu's work had certainly evolved. He used to focus on nudes, during the phase when he was obsessed with the feminine form, as many masters were. Now he'd created pieces with a modern edge.

"What do you think?" he asked her.

"It's good," she said. "Great, actually. I'm really touched by their expressions."

"Life is difficult," he said. "But art has always been there for me. That's what I'm trying to express in this series."

She was moved to see him in this rare moment of vulnerability. What had happened to him over the years? She knew that his father had died from stomach cancer when he was only twenty, and his mother died in a car crash while he was in school. There was always something tragic about Mathieu, a side that Clémence had pitied and wanted to take care of. A part of him was a little boy who needed healing. It was also the part that made him a sensitive and talented artist.

"It's certainly unlike anything you've done before," she said.

He smiled modestly and headed back toward the kitchen. "You want something to drink? I've got some champagne, actually."

"That'd be great. So where's the hand print?"

"It's in my bedroom," he said. "I'll show you in a sec."

He came back with two champagne flutes and handed her one. She brought it to her lips and drank, while feeling his gaze on her. She blushed. The way he was looking at her was making her slightly...dizzy. What was his agenda?

She told herself not to be silly. It had been her idea to come to his place to look at the handprint to begin with.

"It's upstairs," he said. He led her up the grand staircase.

The walls on the second floor were just as bare, except for a funny sketch of a moose and one painting of a boat and a sunset. The subject of the painting wasn't particularly original, but the style seemed familiar.

"I know this artist," she said.

"You do?"

"Didn't we learn about him in school? He was the French painter from Normandy, right? Was a sailor and painted a lot of boats and the sea?"

"Good job," he praised. "You know your stuff."

"But not his name." Clémence scowled, berating herself for not remembering. "It starts with an M..."

"Mercier," he said. "Felix Mercier."

"Right, of course. Is this an original?"

"Yes," he said, flushed with pride, but he quickly added. "Not mine, of course. I wouldn't be able to afford one. It's Gilles's."

"Who is Gilles exactly?"

"He's a financial trader. Part of the reason he wants to room with me is that he wants to learn how to paint. But frankly, he's not very good! He's big on art though. He'll be away in London for another week on a business trip, so he's not around."

"What company does he work for? My boyfriend's in the finance world. Maybe they've crossed paths."

"Oh, I forget." Mathieu made a face. "All those companies sound the same. It's so boring to me."

Clémence agreed, but she did not say so. As much as she loved Arthur, whenever he talked about finance or economics, it went over her head.

Mathieu opened the door to his bedroom. To her surprise, it was neat and sleek, with cream walls. It only contained a desk, a bed, and a bookshelf. When they were living together, one of the things that drove her crazy was that he had been messy— and a hoarder.

"What happened to all your stuff?" Clémence asked.

He chuckled. "As you can tell, my roommate loves minimalist living, so I've been influenced. I mean, why let material possessions drag you down?"

"A financial trader who is not a materialist?" Clémence mused. "I'm learning a lot today."

Mathieu pushed the bed a few inches back. "Check this out. I get chills when I see this."

Clémence crouched down to take a better look. She could see it: a small handprint with a visible palm line.

"Whoever it is must be very, very young," she remarked. "Have you seen this ghost?"

"No. Sometimes I hear a child crying in the middle of the night. At first I thought it was a neighbor, but it's not possible. The family next door does not have a child, and there's nobody living in the other house right now, since they've gone away for the summer. Sometimes I wonder if I'm just having nightmares."

"Definitely creepy. So are you scared to sleep alone?"

"Well, I wouldn't say scared. More like disturbed."

"Let's use the sage. It could help." She was holding the plastic bag, and she reached in to take out one stick to show him. She'd bought another to take home so she could do the same for her apartment, just in case.

"What will it do exactly?"

"We just have to burn it," Clémence said. "The smoke will clear the energy and hopefully get rid of the spirit. You might as well burn the whole thing, to be safe. When I was in Singapore, I met a woman who told me to do this."

"So you've really been traveling a lot, huh?" Mathieu said. "You left right after we broke up. Was our breakup the reason why you went away?"

Clémence felt heat rise to her cheeks. She opened her mouth and was about to deny it, but then thought, *what's the point?* She took out her smartphone and bent down again to take a photo of the handprint.

"Sure. It was hard on me. We were together for so long, and when I found out, I just had to leave."

He put a hand on her shoulder. "I'm so sorry I ever hurt you that way."

"Yes, well, it's okay. I had a great time during those two years. Got to do a lot of new things, meet people, experience different cultures. I'm over it now, and I've moved on."

"So... with your boyfriend now, are you in love with him?"

"Arthur? Yes. He's great..."

But the way he was staring at her made her feel as if he didn't quite believe it. "Are you sure,

Clémence? Take it from me. It's hard to be with someone who's not creative, isn't it? You're an artist. You need someone who understands you."

He was standing looking down at her, as she was still crouched by the mysterious handprint. She looked up at him. Sunlight washed him from behind, making him appear to be a mirage. A small smile was on his shadowed face, a knowing one, as if he still believed that he had her wrapped around his finger.

But she wasn't, was she? She had been over Mathieu for a long time. She didn't feel anything for him now. Sure, he was still as charming as ever, with the complex personality: wounded boy one minute, confident and sensual the next.

"He is creative," she replied. "Arthur plays piano."

She stood up slowly. He didn't say anything. She couldn't maintain eye contact from the intense way he was staring at her. His pale blue eyes were like magnets trying to pull her back in again.

"Let's light this sage," she tried to say in a breezy voice. "Do you have a lighter? The ashes will fall, so we need a plate, too."

She blushed as she talked, feeling stupid for some reason.

"I think there's a lighter in the kitchen," he replied softly.

"Great. Let's start go downstairs and start from the bottom up."

When they reached the top of the stairs, they heard the loud slamming of the front door.

A young woman appeared. She had long brown hair and glinting green eyes. Her face reminded Clémence of a cat. She wore a black designer dress suit, an untucked white blouse, and gold heels, looking stunning. Her eyes narrowed at the sight of Clémence, then at Mathieu. If her eyes were daggers, Clémence would be dead by now.

Chapter 5

"Charlotte." Mathieu clapped his hands together and went down the stairs first. "Don't you have work this afternoon?"

"Nice to see you too," she sniffed. "My boss gave me the afternoon off because the security system had to be changed and the gallery's closed for the rest of the day."

Mathieu approached to give her *bisous*, kisses, on the cheeks, but she went in for a kiss on the mouth.

"This is Clémence," Mathieu introduced her, as Clémence tentatively came down to receive Charlotte.

Clémence wasn't sure whether to go in for a *bisou* greeting. Charlotte didn't look like she was too happy to see her. Even though there was a smile stretched on her face, her piercing green eyes still contained a hint of anger.

"I'm Charlotte, *la copaine* of Mathieu."

Mathieu's girlfriend. Clémence got it. Charlotte looked inquisitively from Clémence to Mathieu as though demanding an explanation.

"Clémence is a friend," Mathieu said.

"I know who she is," Charlotte spat, while maintaining that neutral smile on her face. "Clémence Damour, the heiress of the patisserie chains. You've been in the papers all week."

"*Oui, c'est moi*," Clémence admitted.

"Horrific thing that happened to you and Sophie." She softened just a little. "I've met the Seydoux sisters a couple of times."

"Oh, really?"

"Yes, at gallery openings and things like that. I'm part of that scene too, you know."

"Oh. I didn't. I'm not part of that scene."

"Are you sure?" Charlotte gave a little laugh. "You're the face of the Parisian elite these days."

Mathieu looked from Charlotte to Clémence and quickly jumped in.

"Charlotte works at the Madison Gallery in the sixth arrondissement."

"That's amazing," Clémence exclaimed. "I know that gallery. It's right by our old art school. Are you a curator?"

"Learning to," she said. "I'm an assistant for now, but I'm being primed to take over my boss's position when he retires."

"That's amazing. Mathieu was telling me how important it was to have a creative significant other who shares the same interests. And you must be proud of him, too."

"Oh yes." Charlotte turned her strange smile on Mathieu, who looked uneasy. "He's a star, isn't he? Or he's going to be very soon."

"I thought he was already doing really well," Clémence said.

"Not for the past year and a half," Charlotte said bluntly. "His last couple of shows tanked."

"They just don't get my new work." A harder edge was in Mathieu's voice.

"His last two shows received bad reviews across the board," Charlotte explained.

"Oh, no." Clémence looked at Mathieu. He hadn't told her. He must've been embarrassed. "I'm sorry. If it's any consolation, I think your new pieces are fantastic. They're ahead of your time. Many artists aren't celebrated in their time. Don't let the bad press get you down."

"Thanks, Clémence."

"So, what brings you to Mathieu's place, Clémence?"

"She's just—"

"I'm here to cleanse the house," she said.

"Cleanse?" She raised an eyebrow. "What do you mean?"

"Well, the house seems to be haunted by a small child, so I'm helping him clean the bad energy away with white sage."

She realized how ridiculous that sounded to a logical person, and Charlotte was definitely the logical type.

Charlotte crossed her arms and sneered. "Haunted, huh? Why didn't you just call the Ghostbusters, Mathieu?"

He gave Clémence an apologetic look. "Charlotte doesn't believe in that stuff."

"Don't tell her what *you* think I believe or not," Charlotte said sharply. "If there's a ghost, you should've told me, especially since I spend nearly every night here."

Clémence was getting more and more uncomfortable. There was so much tension in the air. She'd thought her visit was harmless, but obviously Charlotte didn't seem to think so. She hadn't even known that Mathieu was seeing someone. Why didn't he tell her?

"Hey, you know what, guys?" Clémence looked at her watch. "I'd better be going back to work."

"Oh." Mathieu turned to her. "All right. I'll call you some time."

Charlotte glared at him.

"Nice meeting you, Charlotte," Clémence said awkwardly. "*Au revoir.*"

She couldn't leave fast enough.

Chapter 6

"How was your meeting with your ex?" Berenice asked as soon as Clémence entered the Damour kitchen.

"A disaster." Clémence dropped her purse on the corner table and slumped in the seat at their worktable.

Sebastien was working on their seasonal strawberry-and-cream macarons, piping the one-inch shells on a lined tray. Berenice was making their last batch of baguettes for the day.

"I thought things went well earlier in the *salon*," Berenice said. "We saw you two talking and laughing."

"Yes, but I went over to his house later, and his new girlfriend dropped in. It did not go over well. She was pretty pissed off to find me there." She told them all about their run-in with Charlotte.

"Sounds like she's the jealous type," Sebastien said.

"She practically ripped my head off. But I suppose I understand. It doesn't look too good to catch your boyfriend and his ex walking down the stairs from his bedroom. And Mathieu was acting nervous too, so maybe she was even more convinced that something was going on."

"So did anything go on?" Berenice raised an eyebrow.

"No. Of course not. I'm with Arthur. You know that."

"Yeah, but you were pretty crazy about Mathieu for the longest time. You were like a puppy when it came to him."

Clémence sighed. "Yeah, I was pretty pathetic, wasn't I?"

"You don't have to say that twice," Sebastien said curtly.

"Oh, hush," Clémence said.

"Wait, what were you doing at his house, anyway?" Sebastien asked.

Clémence didn't know whether to shudder or laugh as she recalled the reason. "It's the craziest thing." She told them about the ghost child's handprint.

The Soulier siblings looked up at her in disbelief.

"That cannot be true," Sebastien said. "It's absolutely ridiculous."

"I beg to differ," Berenice said. "It could totally be true. Real-life ghost stories happen all the time. What do you think all those horror movies are based on? And Mathieu lives in a house. The chance of it being haunted is pretty high. I mean, France is an old country. I'm pretty sure there are more than a few past residents who've lingered."

"Please," Sebastien said. "Surely you don't believe that."

"Oh, if you were left alone in a creepy old house, you wouldn't be scared?"

"I'd be scared of ax murderers and killers, not ghosts. Even if they were real, they're not tangible. It's not like they can hurt me physically."

Clémence took an almond croissant from one of the cooling trays. She was in a snacking mood. She'd gained five pounds since she'd returned to Paris, but she couldn't help herself when she was in a kitchen surrounded by freshly baked goods. Who could? Nobody asked her to stop, since she was the boss. Besides, she deserved to indulge, especially after surviving the wrath of her ex's new girlfriend.

"This is really amazing," she said between bites. "Why don't I have almond croissants more often? Seriously, has the recipe improved?"

"Not really," Sebastien said. "It's still your parents' original recipe."

"No wonder both the inspector and Mathieu are obsessed with our croissants. I've been pigging out on macarons and éclairs, but I've neglected the croissants for too long."

"I'm glad you still have a passion for sweets," Sebastien said. "For me, it's gotten a bit more mechanical. I eat for work, to perfect and to find fault—not so much for pleasure anymore."

"That's actually kind of sad," Clémence said. "You have to reignite the passion."

Berenice looked at her watch. "Oh, I have to go. I'm starting an outside boot camp class. It's in the Tuileries. You should come sometime." She put the baguettes in the industrial oven. "Keep an eye on these, will you?"

"Sure," Sebastien said.

"Maybe I should go," Clémence said. She hadn't been exercising for a while, and with all the sugar from the desserts in her system, she wasn't the picture of good health. "I'm wiped today, but next time. When is it?"

"The next one's on Friday, if I'm not mistaken. I'll check with the instructor and let you know, so we can go together."

"Great."

After Berenice left, Clémence turned to Sebastien. "You know, Berenice thinks you're gay."

His hazel eyes widened. "She does? Why?"

"Because she thinks you don't have a girlfriend, your best friend is gay, and you have something to hide."

"Just because I have gay friends doesn't mean I'm gay." His mouth twitched into a smile.

"*Je sais*, but you know how Berenice gets. She's easily excited about things. She's preparing for your big coming out. She might even tell your parents."

Sebastien chuckled. "Maya wants to meet my family, so I was planning on introducing her soon, anyway. But in the meantime, I can have some fun with this."

"Why do I regret telling you this now? What are you going to do?"

"Just a little harmless fun."

Chapter 7

Clémence made dinner for Arthur. It was the least she could do. He'd been so great about the whole Mathieu situation. She decided that today would be the last time she saw Mathieu. He could deal with his own ghost, with his own girlfriend.

Arthur rang the bell, and Clémence let him in, greeting him with a big hug and a long kiss. When their lips touched, Clémence felt hesitation from his end. She hoped he was just tired. The circles under his eyes were darker than usual. He'd come home from the library late, having been working on his on PhD on macroeconomics.

"I made salmon and green beans for dinner," she said. "With rice. *Tu as faim?*"

"*Oui*, I'm really hungry. That sounds good."

But Clémence could tell from his expression that he was still distant toward her.

At the table, he poured wine for her. Men always poured wine for women in France. She broke a piece of a fresh Damour baguette for him.

"It certainly smells good," he said. It didn't take long into the meal for him to bring up Mathieu. "How was the rendezvous with your ex? What's his name again?"

"Mathieu," she replied, even though she knew very well that Arthur knew his name.

"So what happened?"

"Um. Well, we talked at Damour. I made him come to the *salon* so the paparazzi wouldn't snap us together out and about—not that we have anything to hide."

"Well, that's funny, because there are pictures of you all over the Internet." He took out his phone from his pocket and showed her a blog post.

The photos were of her and Mathieu outside his house, snapped from earlier that afternoon. They were embracing as she kissed the side of his cheek. The headline said: *Clémence Damour Cheats on Boyfriend with Artist Ex.*

Who could've taken that photo? Was she followed?

"What's going on?" Arthur asked.

"You gotta be kidding me," she said. "I can explain."

He leaned back and crossed his arms. She could tell that he was pissed off. She told him about the ghost story, the child's handprint on his wall, and how she was going to cleanse his house with sage.

"That's pretty hard to believe," he said. "You're pretty naïve if you believe that story."

"Excuse me?" Clémence exclaimed. "Okay, the ghost thing may sound crazy, but why would he lie to me? And there *is* a small handprint on the wall."

"Oh, I don't know, to get you over to his house? To bait you because he knows you're a sucker for anything weird and mysterious? Have you ever thought that maybe the handprint didn't come from an actual ghost?"

"I'm not naïve." Clémence's temper flared. "Look, I understand why you're upset—"

"Do you? This is humiliating. I have friends phoning me up asking me if I'm all right, and even my mother asked me what was going on between us."

"Oh God. I'm sorry. But it's all innocent, I swear."

"Ghosts," Arthur muttered.

"Don't you trust me?"

"Do you trust yourself?"

Clémence blinked. "What? You really think I'm going to cheat on you with Mathieu?"

"Why not? People cheat on each other all the time. If you were close to this guy, who's to say you won't get close again? He'll charm you, pay you a couple of compliments, and you're back in his arms before you know it."

"Do you really think I'm that easy to impress? I don't want him. I swear—"

Just then, the doorbell rang. *Who could it be at this hour?* She wasn't expecting anyone.

"I'll get it," she stood up.

At the front door, she looked through the peephole. Mathieu! Again? He hadn't told her he was stopping by. She considered not answering, but how could she? He'd probably heard her footsteps through the door and—

"Clémence?"

Shoot. He knew she was there. There was no other choice. She had to open up.

"*Bonsoir*, Mathieu. What can I do for you at this hour?"

"I know it's late, but I was in the neighborhood after dining with a gallery owner to talk about my work. Anyway, you left both of your sage sticks, and since I was the in the neighborhood, I figured I'd just return them to you."

"How did you get in downstairs?"

"Someone was coming out. I hope it's all right. I didn't want to intrude. I suppose I also wanted to apologize in person for Charlotte's behavior today. She was just surprised to see you. I hope she didn't hurt your feelings."

"No. It's okay. And one of the sage sticks is for you. Go ahead and use it." She took the other one.

"Charlotte knows a lot about you. It's because I mention you a lot, especially during the past week, when stories about you were just everywhere. I guess she got a little jealous."

"It's understandable. No hard feelings."

"Hey—is that an original de Kooning?"

Mathieu brushed past Clémence and entered the apartment's hallway to look at an abstract charcoal sketch of a woman by the famous Dutch artist. Clémence didn't know how to stop him.

"Er, yeah. It's an original. My mother's. She won it at an auction at Christie's."

"Do you mind if we turn on the lights? I want to take a better look."

Clémence whispered, "Actually, Mathieu, I'm sorry, but this isn't a good time—"

"*Bonsoir.*" Arthur approached.

Mathieu turned to him and put on his smoothest grin. "I'm Mathieu Leroy, Clémence's...friend."

"Arthur Dubois." He reluctantly shook his hand.

"This is Arthur, my boyfriend that I told you about," Clémence said awkwardly.

"Anyway, I'm just dropping by to return something Clémence left at my house earlier, since I was in the neighborhood. Hope you don't mind."

"Not at all," Arthur said through gritted teeth. "I heard you're an artist."

"That's right."

"I think I read about you recently—about one of your shows."

"Well, chances are you read a bad review, but as Clémence reassured me earlier today, my new works are the stuff of genius. And the public will finally realize it someday. Maybe when I'm dead, right?" He chuckled, then something caught his attention. "Hey—I remember this painting."

It was an oil painting of pink flamingos. "Clémence painted it ages ago," Mathieu mused.

"You did?" Arthur looked at her. "You didn't tell me you did it."

"Frankly, I'm a bit embarrassed by it," Clémence said. "There's a lot of mistakes. See these brush strokes? And how the black paint mixed with the pink?"

"It's beautiful," said Arthur. "I can't believe you didn't tell me."

"Clémence was always modest about her work," Mathieu said. "But she's talented, all right. Maybe more so than I am."

She blushed. She'd never heard Mathieu say that. It meant a lot to her—even though she didn't quite believe what he said was true.

"Your parents have an amazing collection of art, as always," Mathieu remarked. "Arthur, I hear you're in finance."

"Sort of. I'm working on my PhD right now, in macroeconomics, and I'm working at a consulting firm part-time."

"Macroeconomics? I really know nothing about it."

"I'm sure you're more creative than a numbers man, and it's probably not very interesting to you."

"That's not true," said Mathieu, even though Clémence knew it was. "I just don't understand it."

The three of them didn't say anything further. Clémence stood close to Arthur. She wanted Mathieu to leave but was too polite to say so. She hoped he could take a hint.

"Well, I didn't mean to disrupt your evening," Mathieu finally said. "I better be going."

"Okay, thanks for bringing the sage back," Clémence said. "Hope it'll work in your home."

"Let's hope." Mathieu crossed his fingers.

"Pesky, those ghosts, huh?" Arthur remarked.

"I don't know what would be worse: if the handprint were real or if somebody went out of their way to play a practical joke on me. Well, bonne soirée."

Before leaving, Mathieu gave Clémence a *bisou* on each cheek, and shook Arthur's hand again.

"That was awkward," Clémence said, after she closed the door.

Arthur didn't reply. He only went back into the kitchen. Clémence followed.

Their dinner, half eaten, was cold.

"I've lost my appetite," Arthur said.

He opened the door in the kitchen that led to the servant's staircase and went up the stairs. While Arthur's family lived on the third floor, he took a servant's room on the seventh.

"Wait, Arthur."

He didn't turn back. He kept walking up the steps as his footsteps echoed on the staircase.

Chapter 8

Clémence stuffed a piece of *pain au chocolat* into her mouth. Lately she'd been eating more than she'd been baking. Ever since the kidnapping, she'd been binge eating like crazy. She'd never been an emotional eater, but it was never too late to start. It was the stress. Now that Arthur was mad at her, she needed comforting more than ever.

"Are you okay?" Sebastien gave her a strange look.

"I look like *merde*, don't I?" Clémence certainly felt like a mess.

After Arthur left the night before, she had polished off the rest of the wine and begun crying. It wasn't just their fight that caused the breakdown—it was everything. *Maybe I should call Sophie Seydoux and get the name of her therapist,* she thought.

"Take it easy on that pastry," Sebastien said.

"Too much alcohol and too many sweets," she muttered. "I can cut the alcohol, but not sure about the sweets."

"Put down the *pain au chocolat* and let's get back to work."

"Fine. I need to get my shit together, don't I?

Sebastien was working on the apricot-and-melon macaron for their fruity summer macaron collection.

"Well, I have been doing most of the inventing lately," he said.

"How was the banana macaron?"

"See for yourself. It's coming out of the oven, and I'm making the coconut filling. I think I've finally perfected it."

Since the shells needed to cool before they could pipe on the filling, she busied herself helping Sebastien improve the starfruit recipe.

As she started to work, she began to relax. This was what she loved about being in the kitchen. There was something soothing about weighing the ingredients, mixing them together, and watching the colors change. A few simple ingredients could make the most delicious, decadent, and beautiful treat. That was the joy: the transformation from the ordinary to the extraordinary.

Unlike painting, working in a kitchen wasn't something she struggled with. Even perfecting the recipes through multiple attempts was still fun. Maybe it was because she didn't need to prove to herself in this field. There was little pressure, and the enjoyment factor was high.

When she'd seen Mathieu's new paintings, she'd rediscovered how much she wanted to be a painter. Even though the art world couldn't see it now, she was certain his work had merit and that he was going to go places. Mathieu had something to say, and he was not the type to compromise artistic integrity. She had meant it when she said that his work was brilliant. Although they'd had some personal conflict, she respected him, one artist to another.

Seeing how productive Mathieu was, how persistent, Clémence felt she could do more. A lot more. She was too stuck in her comfort zone to pursue her big passion. She'd barely gotten started on her series of dessert paintings. The one and only painting she'd worked on was of the pistachio macaron, and she hadn't been to an art class at the Spinoza Atelier since she started investigating Sophie's kidnapping.

The teacher and her peers couldn't blame her for taking some time off, but she couldn't make excuses to herself anymore. She needed to get her life back on track. There were no more murders, no more ex-boyfriends, no more chaos to get in the way.

Mentally, she made a list of all the things she needed to straighten out:

One: The issue with Arthur. A non-issue really. She wouldn't see Mathieu from now on. If he contacted her again, she'd respect Arthur enough to say no. His girlfriend Charlotte would also appreciate their lack of contact. Arthur was still mad, but she couldn't see why he wouldn't forgive her when she proved how much she loved him. Maybe she'd give him a full-body massage that night, and feed him some fresh-made macarons.

Two: Restrict to eating only one dessert a day. Then one every two days. Stop grabbing junk to eat on the go, and consume more vegetables. If she needed to, she could get her chefs to make her healthy meals to take home.

Three: Exercise. Go to bootcamp with Berenice. Maybe she could even start taking self-defense classes. It would definitely come in handy.

Four: Go back to her art classes, starting tomorrow. No more excuses. It didn't matter if she wasn't as talented as Mathieu or other artists. She had to push herself to do what she loved.

The macaron mix was done, and she smiled in pride. She scooped the mixture into a piping bag then piped perfect one-inch circles on a lined tray.

She felt better already, making the macarons and a checklist.

Sebastien began piping the coconut cream on the cooled banana macaron shells and sandwiching them together. Clémence helped. Making macarons was a simple kind of happiness, like enjoying a beautiful garden, or wearing nice clothes.

"Try one," Sebastien said.

When she bit into the banana-coconut macaron, the flavors exploded in her mouth. It was melt-in-her-mouth delicious, as all Damour macarons were.

"Amazing."

"That's why they pay me the big bucks," Sebastien said.

"So what's the deal with you and Maya? Have you told Berenice and your family yet?"

"No, but Berenice came over to my place yesterday, and I made sure I left a pair of leather chaps on the coffee table for her to comment on." Sebastien chuckled at the memory.

"Did she ask you about it?"

"Of course. She's nosy. I told her I had them because I was going to a leather bar in the Marais."

The Marais was a gay-friendly neighborhood in central Paris. "What did she say?"

"She asked me if I was gay. I said I wasn't, but that I was going to this leather bar."

"How did she take that?"

"She didn't believe me. She wanted to come to the bar, but I told her females weren't allowed."

"Discrimination. What are you doing with leather chaps, anyway? You bought them just for the joke?"

"No. They're Ted's. Why would I buy leather chaps?"

"So aren't you afraid Berenice is going to tell your parents? Aren't they pretty religious?"

Sebastien smiled slyly. "She'll probably tell them. It'll be good for them. I want to be there to film their reactions."

"You're cruel," Clémence said. "In the most delicious way."

"I'm not a baker for nothin'. They always have their noses in my personal life. I'll give them what they deserve. I like to see them sweat."

"Speaking of sweating, are you making any progress in your ballet class?"

"Not really," Sebastien said. "I'm sick of doing pliés. Maya loves it, but I think I'm going to bail."

"Well, you don't need to do something you don't enjoy just because your girlfriend's into it."

"Maya's into doing things together in general. Maybe I'll just invite her to do one of the things I enjoy."

"Such as?"

"Watching football." *Soccer.*

"I'm sure she'll be riveted," she said sarcastically.

"A new sports bar just opened up near my place."

"What a romantic experience that would be for a young couple. Hey, why don't you just play football with her? Like, on a co-ed team."

She saw cogs turning in his head. "Hmm. That's not a bad idea."

"It makes sense. She sounds like a doer, and you sound like...the opposite of that. How did you meet, anyway?"

"My friend Ted. He was the one who introduced us. She's his sister's friend—"

A loud cough interrupted their conversation. Inspector Cyril St. Clair stood by the doorway. Caroline, the manager, came up beside him looking apologetic.

"He wanted to see you and I couldn't stop him." Caroline said to Clémence. "Sorry."

"You're lucky I didn't bring my officers with me," Cyril said. "With all the paparazzi outside your door, Damour, that would give them something to talk about."

"What do you want, Cyril?" Clémence was on a first-name basis with the incompetent inspector, with whom she'd never seen eye to eye.

"Oh you don't know? Another murder, and it involves another one of your products—surprise, surprise. And you know what else is surprising? It involves you."

The inspector was in his mid-thirties, he had a hawk-like nose, cold green eyes, and a crude smile. He was insolent, short-tempered, and overly sarcastic. She was used to his behavior, but it didn't mean she tolerated him.

Clémence sighed. "Caroline, can we use your office, please?"

"Go ahead," she replied. "I'll be out on the floor."

Caroline gave Cyril a sharp look before turning back to the *salon de thé*.

Clémence took off her apron and led Cyril into the office. She closed the door.

"What's going on now?" she asked. "Another murder? Are you kidding me?"

"Murder is never a joke," he said dryly. "After grilling Mathieu Leroy yesterday, I really wouldn't be surprised if you had something to do with this."

Clémence shook her head. "Wait. Start from the beginning."

"Charlotte Lagrange was murdered last night. At first we thought it was a suicide, since she was shot in the head. She was found lying facedown in her apartment with a gun next to her. But in fact, neighbors heard her scream before the gun was fired at about eight p.m. It's a strange thing, actually. Someone killed her for sure, because neighbors reported hearing a door close after the gunshot, which meant the murderer simply exited her apartment and went out as if he or she was just paying a visit."

"And nobody saw who it was?"

Cyril shrugged and looked at her wryly. "It could be you."

"I'll have you know that I was at home with my boyfriend at around that time."

"I know. Your ex-boyfriend told me. I was interrogating him, and he said he was at a business dinner."

"That's what he told me."

"So he *did* go to your house after?"

"Yes."

"That checks out, then. Mathieu Leroy is innocent."

"But why would someone kill Charlotte?"

"That's what I'm trying to find out."

"Is that why you're here?" Clémence put her hands on her hips. She broke into a cocky smile. "You want me to help you, don't you?"

"Don't flatter yourself, Damour. I wanted to break the news that we found another one of your pastries at the crime scene. You know what was in Charlotte's kitchen? An uneaten almond croissant from your patisserie."

"Oh."

"What did I tell you? Your products are cursed."

"Hey, you didn't eat the croissant, did you?" Clémence joked. "I know you love those almond croissants."

He responded with a stern look. "I'll eat another croissant from Damour when I want to get shot."

Clémence let out a fake gasp. "Surely you don't mean that."

Cyril pulled out a picture of Charlotte's dead body. She was lying facedown on her apartment floor, her dark hair spread out like a fan. Blood pooled around her, and a gun was lying beside her right hand.

"I thought you'd like a challenge, Damour. As soon as you found out about Charlotte, I figured you would try to get your greedy little hands on the perp, but I want to propose a little contest. This time, I'm going to catch the murderer, not you."

"Your ego's pretty shattered, huh?" Clémence had solved quite a few cases already. She'd been outsmarting Cyril ever since she returned to Paris. *You want a showdown?* she thought. *You got one.*

"You're lucky you have an alibi," Cyril said.

"What do you mean, lucky? I don't need luck if I didn't do it. You know I didn't."

"Fine. So who did?"

"If you're smart, who do *you* think did it?"

"Well, it's quite obvious that—" Cyril stopped and narrowed his eyes at her. "Nice try."

"You have no clue, do you?" Clémence said. "I'll definitely figure it out before you do." Mathieu must've been devastated. She felt bad for the part she'd played in upsetting Charlotte during her final day on earth. "I know the people involved, and I'm going to do them justice."

"Justice is my middle name," Cyril said. "You've been embarrassing me for too long. This time, I'll show you who the real investigator is in this city."

"You embarrass yourself, Cyril. If you did your job properly, you wouldn't need me. Now can you please leave? I'm at work."

"When I win, I get a week's free lunch at Damour," Cyril said. "With champagne."

"Is that a death wish?" Clémence chuckled. "Fine. And if I win?"

"Very unlikely, but what do you want?"

"A personalized letter from you to me, admitting how crap you are as an inspector and how superior I am. Don't worry—I'll give you a rough outline. You also need to sign it so I can frame it. Deal?"

Cyril rolled his eyes, but he assented. "Deal."

They shook hands.

Chapter 9

"Sorry, Sebastien," Clémence said when she returned to the kitchen. "Duty calls. I'll have to leave you to the macarons. Ask Berenice to help when she gets in."

"Another murder?" he asked. "They're really becoming a regular thing around here now, huh?"

"Tell me about it."

She tried calling Arthur, but he didn't answer. Was he ignoring her on purpose? She left a message saying that she wanted to speak to him and that it was urgent. She wanted to explain what she was about to do. She had to see Mathieu again to get more information about Charlotte's death.

Mathieu was the person she called next.

"Allô?"

"Mathieu. How are you doing?"

"Not particularly well.

"I heard about Charlotte," Clémence said. "I'm so sorry. The inspector paid me a visit."

"I'm still in shock."

"I know. Listen, can we meet?"

"I suppose. I'm at home."

"Great. I'll come by."

When she rushed outside, the paps aimed their cameras at her.

"Clémence, are you cheating on Arthur with your ex?"

"How does Arthur feel about all this?"

"Didn't your ex cheat on you?"

A horrifying realization came to her. If the paps were harassing her with these kinds of questions, they were probably doing the same to Arthur.

She wished she could make it up to him, but there was another murder case to solve. She had to go to Mathieu's house. Surely Arthur would understand once she explained everything.

Clémence quickly got into a taxi to escape the paparazzi. Luckily there were always plenty of taxis lined up at Place du Trocadéro. Traffic wasn't too bad that time of day, and she was able to reach Les Lilas in less than half an hour. She really hoped she wouldn't be photographed in front of his house again.

When Mathieu answered the door, he looked terrible. He hadn't shaved and his eyes were bloodshot. He was nursing a glass of gin. Nevertheless, he gave Clémence a big hug that felt heavy with need.

"Are you okay?" she asked.

"Terrible. What a gruesome night."

"What exactly happened?"

"When I got home last night, I got a call from the police saying that Charlotte had been shot dead earlier that evening. The police took me in for questioning, and I was there until two a.m. The inspector really wanted to lock me up, but I had an airtight alibi. I was at the restaurant with the gallery owner, as I told you. They questioned him, as well as the restaurant workers. Luckily, the restaurant had security cameras, so there was proof that I was there. It all checked out. If I'd been home alone or something, who knows what the police would've done to me?"

"They're brutal, aren't they?" Clémence said sympathetically. "Do you have any idea why anyone would kill Charlotte?"

He shook his head. "It's so odd. Charlotte was a sweet girl. I mean, sure, she was a little feisty when you met her, but she's not usually like that. I have to admit that we've only been dating for a month, so I don't know everything about her." Mathieu downed the rest of his gin. "I feel horrible. Yesterday she was really upset about, well, us. She has a bit of a jealous streak. It was all my fault, and I apologized for hours. In the end, I think she forgave me, and she even took one of the croissants home, so I don't think she was that upset about us by the end."

That would've explained why Charlotte had a Damour croissant in her kitchen. Clémence couldn't scope out Charlotte's apartment because the police were over there, even though she would've like to. Her only hope was to find out more about Charlotte's life.

"What else can you tell me about her?" she asked Mathieu.

"Charlotte wanted to be a top art curator at a prestigious gallery. That's why we had such a connection. We met at an art show, and we had an instant rapport. We were both ambitious and passionate about art. She's from Strasbourg, but she moved over here for work."

Strasbourg? The girl had an entire life in Strasbourg. Who knew what kind of people from her past could have done this to her? Clémence sighed.

"Did she ever mention anybody she didn't get along with in Strasbourg?"

"I don't know. Her family seems very normal. I even visited them once. Everything about her is normal. If anything, she'd rather live there. She hates Paris. If it weren't for the job opportunities here, she'd live in Strasbourg with her family. I wonder if it was just a deranged psychopath who broke into her home. I wouldn't be surprised if it was just a random shooting from a sadistic weirdo. I hope she wasn't in a lot of pain, and that nothing else happened..."

Clémence remembered the photo that the inspector had shown her. Charlotte's clothes had been on. She'd still had on her tight black dress pants and matching blazer. She hadn't been touched inappropriately, from what Clémence could tell.

"No, she hadn't. Somebody just wanted her dead. It's the most peculiar thing. Why?"

Mathieu shrugged. "I guess I'll let the inspector figure it out."

"Come on. The whole team is pretty incompetent. You know the Paris police—are they ever on the ball?"

Mathieu sighed. "I suppose not, but there's nothing I can do."

"Yes, there is. *I'm* good at solving mysteries. I can help you find the killer."

Mathieu looked up at her in surprise. "Really?"

"Sure. I've helped the inspector solve a number of crimes already." She knew she was bragging a little, but she had to state her case. "Of course, I'm not guaranteeing anything, but I'll give it my best shot. What about her workplace? Are there coworkers or clients who she didn't get along with?"

"Nothing that I'm aware of. It all seems pretty harmonious there. She was going to be promoted, and the only thing she liked about this city was her workplace—and me."

"Has she ever stepped on anyone's toes to get to where she is now?"

"She's very talented, beautiful, and confident. I wouldn't be surprised if people were jealous of her. But I don't know who would be competing with her. If anybody hated her enough to want her dead, maybe Charlotte wouldn't even have a clue."

"What about you? What about your ex-girlfriend?"

Mathieu's eyes widened. "You think Sarah could be a killer?"

"I'm not saying anything. I'm just trying to cover all the bases."

"Sarah and I have a friendly relationship. We still keep in touch."

"Why did you break up?"

"We were just better off as friends. Our relationship petered out when we realized how different we were. That was eight months ago. I met Charlotte last month and felt she was a better fit for me. Like I said, it's better to be with someone who understands art, you know?"

"So what is Sarah doing now?"

"She does a few lingerie shoots for catalogs once in a while, but she also has a part-time job at one of Galeries Lafayette's perfume booths."

"Hmm. Does she have an online social media presence?"

"She has a Facebook fan page for her modeling."

Clémence searched her name on her smart-phone. The girl didn't have a lot of fans, that was for sure—only ninety likes. She'd used to feel resentment toward Sarah for stealing Mathieu away more than two years ago, but the girl was now a salesgirl, and her career was going nowhere. Clémence couldn't help but pity her.

Unless, of course, she had killed Charlotte.

Chapter 10

After talking to Mathieu for another hour, she returned home and continued studying Sarah's Facebook page on her laptop. Miffy barked at her heels in the kitchen.

"I know you want to walk, Miff, but I have to do some research right now. Can you wait?"

Miffy looked as if she understood. She began playing with a rubber dog bone in the corner. Clémence turned back to Sarah's modeling photos. She was a gorgeous redhead with creamy skin, but her body shape was too curvy, not ideal for the stick-thin world of modeling. While she was incredibly beautiful, there was something awkward about her poses, as if she wasn't in complete control of her features or her body, and as if she wasn't entirely comfortable being in front of the camera.

Clémence looked through Sarah's friends list to see if they had any mutual friends. Mathieu was on it, of course. There were some names that Clémence vaguely recognized, but she wanted to find someone she knew well.

She thought about approaching Sarah herself, but there was less of a chance that she'd open up to her. Clémence preferred to ask a mutual friend to probe Sarah with questions.

Just when she was about to give up on Sarah's list of three thousand friends, she came across Madeleine Seydoux's name.

She'd met Madeleine only recently after the whole debacle with Madeleine's sister's kidnapping. They'd reached out to each other several times in the past week. The kidnapping incident had bonded the girls in the short amount of time they'd known each other. Clémence figured she was the perfect person to ask.

When she pulled out her smartphone from her purse to make the call, she realized that she had two missed calls from Arthur, as well as a text message.

The message was simply a link. She clicked on it. It led to a gossip website, *Paris Social*, which had a special focus on Paris celebrities and socialites. This particular post featured a picture of her entering Mathieu's house, taken earlier that day. Mathieu was embracing her. The headline read: *Clémence Damours returns to ex for the second time, cheats on boyfriend.*

Clémence felt heat rising in her body. *Anger.* She was angry at the paparazzi scum who captured an innocent moment, and at Arthur for simply believing everything he read.

She immediately called Arthur. He didn't pick up and she had to leave a message.

"Arthur, please, *please* don't believe what they're writing. It's not true. I'm not cheating on you. The reason I went to visit Mathieu today was because his girlfriend was murdered last night. I'll explain everything. Call me when you get this. Maybe you can help me? Just call me, please."

He had to understand why she had to get involved. He *would* understand, wouldn't he?

Next, she called Madeleine. She thought Madeleine might've been busy with work, but she picked up.

"Clémence, hello," she answered brightly. "What's new?"

"Well, actually, I'm in a bit of a pickle." She explained about Mathieu's girlfriend being killed.

"Oh, my God. Charlotte Lagrange. I've met her. How sad!"

"Did you know her well?"

"We've had a few conversations—you know, party small talk. So no, we weren't close, but I can't believe she was killed!"

"What would you guys talk about?"

"Mostly fashion, art—things like that. I don't remember exactly. I talk to so many people at parties, although I did remember that she dressed to the nines when she came out. That girl had style."

"Do you know of any enemies she might have had?"

"Hmm. I have no idea. You know how bitchy some of the other girls can get. I'm sure there were some who hated on her guts, but I really hope none of them would hate her enough to kill her!"

"It's what I'm trying to find out," Clémence said.

"Poor Mathieu. I hope he's all right."

"The thing is, I'm investigating a lead."

"Really?" Madeleine exclaimed. "Who?"

"I hope you don't take offence to this, but it's Sarah. Sarah Jones. She's a friend of yours, right?"

"Yes. Sarah. She used to come to parties with Mathieu, and that's how we became friends. She was an up-and-coming model, right? We weren't too close, either, but we used to see each other at parties all the time, and she seemed like a nice girl, if a little timid. But she stopped going to parties a while ago. I haven't seen her for months. Actually, I can't remember the last time I saw her."

"Why do you think she stopped coming?"

"I don't know. She was tagging along with Mathieu at those things to begin with. I don't think she enjoyed the spotlight. She was always by his side. Her confidence didn't seem to be too high, and I always felt a bit bad for her so I'd try to talk to her and include her in conversation."

"What do you know about her?"

"She's Irish. She moved to Paris to study French literature, but she didn't graduate because a modeling scout found her and she signed on to an agency. For a while, she was doing well with lingerie campaigns. The only thing really striking about her is her beauty. Unfortunately, she doesn't seem to have the personality to really succeed in the business. Plus she'd gained a bit of weight the last time I saw her. I mean, she looks fine in real life, but it didn't fly in the fashion industry. But she's a sweet girl. I don't think she would've murdered Charlotte."

"Who knows?" Clémence said. "Appearances can be deceiving. I really want to question her, but I was wondering if you can help me. She knows who I am, and I doubt she'd want to open up to me. Can you do me a favor and reach out to her? Ask her if she wants to have a quick coffee or something? I want to find out where she was last night, when the shooting happened. The murder is in the papers, but Charlotte wasn't named in the articles, so it's not common knowledge. She won't suspect that you know that Charlotte's dead. Are you up for it?"

"Sure. Sounds fun. I always wanted to be a spy, like in the movies! I can see if Sarah's available tonight for a quick drink. Are you going to have me wear a wire?"

Clémence chuckled. "I'm not so high tech. When you meet her, just call me and leave your phone on. I'll tape your conversation from my end of the phone."

"Oh, even better. It'll be so much fun!"

Chapter 11

Madeleine called back twenty minutes later to inform Clémence that Sarah had been pleased to hear from her. She'd agreed to meet up with Madeleine in a small café in the 9th arrondissement near Galeries Lafayette, where she was working that day.

As Clémence and Madeleine chatted about their plan, Clémence went on Google Maps and saw that there was a *crêperie* across the street from the café, where she could watch Sarah without being seen. She told Madeleine to try to get a table outside.

It was past two, and she still hadn't received a call back from Arthur. Surely he'd had time to call her during lunch. She left another message on his voicemail, telling him that she was going to be out investigating and didn't know what time she would be home.

She changed into all black: her spy outfit. She'd been wearing a lot of black recently, as if that would help her blend in with the shadows. She brought her black sun hat for good measure, to hide her trademark bob. This way Sarah wouldn't be able to recognize her from across the street.

Clémence had met Sarah briefly after Mathieu dumped her. One day she'd dropped unannounced by the apartment that she used to share with Mathieu, to pick up some things that she'd left after she moved out. Sarah had been hanging around. Clémence wouldn't have been surprised if Sarah had already moved in to replace her. It'd been a dramatic experience for Clémence, to say the least. While Sarah had been soft-spoken and polite, Clémence still hated her. She resented her long, luscious hair, her Scarlett Johansson curves, her pouty lips, and how Mathieu was simply obsessed with her.

Mathieu was a charmer. He could flit from girl to girl like a bee flitted between flowers.

Of course, he dropped Sarah in the end, when the novelty wore off. In that, Clémence sympathized with Sarah.

On the front steps of the Palais Garnier, she waited for Madeleine to show up. Clémence had told her that she'd be dressed in black, in case she failed to recognize her.

A cab pulled up, and Madeleine stepped out and waved to Clémence with a big smile. The eldest Seydoux sister had long brown hair styled in loose waves, large doe eyes, and porcelain skin. She wore a soft pink designer pants suit, a silk cream blouse, and black Louboutin heels, looking every inch the chic working girl-slash-socialite she was.

"So good to see you!" Madeleine greeted her with *bisous*. "No pesky paparazzi at your back today?"

"Nope. Good riddance."

"All this extra attention is draining Sophie, too. She can't go to therapy without being harassed. But she's making the most out of it. She signed a book deal to tell her story. Maybe it'll be therapeutic for her. I heard they asked you too, but you said no."

"There's nothing to tell."

"You're modest. You saved her life."

"Oh, it's pure luck." Clémence waved her compliment away. "Anyway, you're looking fab."

"Speak for yourself, fashionista. You were Best Dressed on the Paris Social blog this month. They love you."

"Well, they've been a pain in the ass." She explained how they'd managed to snap her going into her ex's house two days in a row.

"They're just desperate for a good scoop. At least the paps aren't around right now, but let's get walking, since this is a photo hotspot."

"So Sarah said she was coming at five thirty p.m.?" Clémence asked.

Madeleine nodded. "That's what she agreed to. She says she has a break from work at that time. I don't know what to expect. I haven't seen her in ages. It might even be a year. Time passes so fast."

"The important thing is to ask her what she thinks about Mathieu's new girlfriend, and also to find out what she was doing last night."

"Got it. God, what if she's actually the murderer? I mean, I'd be talking to a murderer, then!"

"We'll see. We don't know anything, so we can't jump to conclusions. Who knows? Maybe she might know something about Mathieu and Charlotte that nobody else does. Just ask questions, without sounding like you're interrogating her."

"It's okay. I'm the nosy type and she knows it, so she won't suspect anything out of the ordinary."

"I figured you'd be the perfect person for this gig." Clémence smiled. "You'll be a good partner-in-crime."

They reached the café that was on a side street from Galerie Lafayette.

"Perfect," Clémence said. "There are plenty of empty seats outside. I'll be inside that *crêperie*, watching from the window. Call me as soon as she comes, and leave the phone on."

The girls took their places and waited. Madeleine lit a cigarette and smoked, along with everybody else who was sitting outside. There were still fifteen minutes to go until Sarah would show up, so Madeleine played around on her smartphone.

Clémence was tempted to order a chocolate crêpe. But she'd already eaten a *pain au chocolat* that day, so per her one-dessert-a-day limit, she settled on a glass of freshly squeezed orange juice.

When she'd drunk most of the juice, Sarah finally showed up in gray pants and a white dress shirt. Clémence could see Sarah had gained a little bit of weight. Was this why she wasn't modeling as much anymore? Her long hair was tied into a bun, and her face was made up; Sarah was still just as beautiful as Clémence remembered.

Madeleine called her on the phone. Clémence muted her phone and started recording the conversation.

Madeleine and Sarah made a fuss greeting each other, making small talk and complimenting one another, as Clémence had done with Madeleine earlier. The waiter took their drink orders, and Madeline immediately turned back to Sarah, "It's been so long. How have you been? *Where* have you been?"

Sarah shrugged, a weary smile on her face. "Oh, you know. I'm still modeling, but I found it a little desensitizing. I'm disillusioned with it. In fact, I grew to hate it. I've tried it for a good year and a half in Paris, but it's not the career for me."

"Why not?"

"I don't know. I hate being treated like a clothes hanger. Or a piece of meat. Sometimes I have to go to castings, and they ask me to strip on the spot."

"What about acting? That's at least a little bit more humanizing."

"Well, I'm not good in front of the cameras. I can't act. You know how shy I am. Plus, I'm Irish. My French is not the best. To do that I'd have to go to the UK, move altogether."

"So why don't you? Unless there's someone keeping you here."

"No." Sarah laughed. "I'm going through kind of a dry spell, actually."

"Nobody at all? A gorgeous girl like you? Are you still hung up on Mathieu?"

"No. We're better off apart."

"I heard he's moved on with some girl who works at an art gallery or something," Madeleine said. "You're not a teensy bit jealous?"

"Our relationship just wasn't meant to be. I felt it. Sure, I'm a bit hurt that he's moved on so fast, but I want him to be happy. I'm sure I'll meet someone when I'm ready for it, too."

"That's very big of you. Every time I go through a breakup, I'm batshit crazy for weeks, driving everyone around me nuts."

Sarah laughed. "Well, it's not easy, you know? But I try to be mature about it. Mathieu seems happy, so I'll just let him be. Like my mother says, when God closes a door, He opens a window."

"Well, who needs guys? What have you been doing for fun lately?"

"Actually, I've been pretty busy. To tell you the truth, there's been a change in my life. It's big, and it's partly why I haven't been going out at all."

Madeleine leaned in. "What is it?"

"I had a baby."

"What? No way!"

Sarah nodded. "Yes. She's my pride and joy. She's nearly one. I'm lucky that she got into crèche so I'm able to work part-time. Her name is Joy. Do you want to see pictures?"

Clémence was stunned. If Sarah had the baby a year ago, then that meant the father was...

"Is she Mathieu's?" Madeleine asked.

"Yes."

"Oh my gosh! How is it being a single mother?"

"It's okay. I'm working at Galeries Lafayette because I want to. I know it doesn't sound glamorous, but I like it. At least I get to talk to people. It keeps me sane. I'd rather move back to Ireland, but Mathieu needs to be here, and I want my daughter to know her father. He's had some setbacks, but he says he's going to get a big break soon so he can take care of us better."

"Right. His career hasn't done as well as we all predicted."

"He's certain something big is going to happen soon, though. He says in the next few months, he'll be wealthy enough to hire a nanny and help me rent a bigger apartment, since Joy lives with me. He really wants us to stay in Paris. I was seriously considering moving back to Ireland before he convinced me. That's where my family is, and I'd get more help, but I trust Mathieu."

"What does his big break entail?"

"Another show, I suppose. He said his roommate Gilles is helping him with something. He has connections in the art world or something."

Clémence still couldn't believe it. Mathieu was a father? Why hadn't he told her?

Chapter 12

Clémence was still in shock when Arthur finally called her back.

"Hey, Clémence. Are you okay? What exactly is going on?"

Sarah had returned to work at the perfume counter at Galeries Lafayette. After checking in with Clémence, Madeleine had a rendezvous to get to, and Clémence had left as well.

"I'm fine," she said. "I'm walking on Boulevard Haussman."

"I'm sorry I didn't call back until now. I was too mad at you to listen to your voicemail. I didn't know that Mathieu's girlfriend was killed."

"When are you going home? Let's talk in person."

"I'm at the library, but I don't think I can do any more work today. I'll meet you at the apartment, then. What were you up to today?"

"Checking up on a lead. She wasn't the killer, but I found out something interesting. Tell you about it later."

"Okay, I'll meet you back at home in twenty minutes."

As Clémence passed the serial shoppers on the Boulevard Haussman holding shopping bags from high-end retailers, she tried to figure out why Mathieu hadn't told her he had a daughter. Why was it a secret? Was it because he didn't want to hurt her further? Maybe he knew she'd once had the desire to marry him and start a family together—back when she was young and naïve, and when she was still in love with Mathieu.

She wanted answers from him. But first she had to be with Arthur. He was the man she loved, and she wanted him back on her side again.

Clémence took the Métro back to Trocadéro Station. The paparazzi weren't in front of 4 Place du Trocadéro this time. They probably got tired of waiting around for her and gave up. Maybe the best thing she could do was not show up for work. They'd get bored by the waiting and hopefully they'd just stop coming altogether.

As she turned onto Avenue Kléber, she spotted Arthur walking just twenty feet ahead. She instantly recognized the back of his head, the swirl of his hair.

She resisted the temptation to run up and announce her presence, and she maintained her pace to continue watching him from afar. But as he punched in the code to unlock the iron door to the building, she couldn't help but run up and hug him from behind.

"Clémence," he exclaimed in surprise. He slowly turned around in her arms.

"Hey you." She gave him a sheepish smile. They'd been together only the day before, when they'd had that awkward fight, but it felt as if it had been forever since she'd seen him. She wasn't used to sleeping in an empty bed anymore.

He let go of the door and faced her. The sun was setting, and the Eiffel Tower was a dusty rose in the distance. He cupped her face and kissed her passionately. Pedestrians passed by, but she didn't care. She didn't even care if they were being photographed.

Clémence melted in his arm. This was why she loved him. His unfailing support and his warmth. His trust in her. Not to mention that he smelled good and was sexy as hell.

"Come on," he said. "Let's go home."

In the tiny elevator, which was barely big enough for two people, they entangled themselves, furiously making out. No words were needed. By the time the doors opened, they were out of breath and at a loss for words anyway.

Their relationship was new, but it felt as though they'd known each other forever. They fought before their romance had even begun, so it was only natural to make up just as easily. It was also natural to get jealous once in a while. The complications came as part of a committed relationship. They'd make it work as long they both made the other feel special and loved on a regular basis.

"I'm sorry about everything," Clémence said. "I got caught up in my own curiosity, as usual, and consideration of how you were feeling was left in the back burner."

"It's okay, Clémence. I think I might have overreacted."

Clémence was surprised by the softness of his tone. "Really?"

He nodded. "Mathieu's girlfriend was killed. That changes things. Of course you'd want to get involved and help."

"I wasn't trying to hurt you. I swear, I don't have feelings for Mathieu. Of course, I care about him as a friend, and I want to help him figure out who could do this to Charlotte."

He looked into her eyes, still cupping her face. "I believe you." He kissed the top of her forehead.

She slid the key into her apartment door and punched in the code to turn off the alarm. Miffy greeted them, and Clémence gave her a bit of attention before settling in.

In the living room, Arthur poured himself a glass of whiskey. Clémence nursed a cup of water. They sank into the red couches. A chandelier hung over them. There was a nonworking fireplace and a modern painting of Katherine Hepburn above it. Clémence and her mother both loved the legendary actress.

She filled Arthur in on everything: the inspector's visit, Madeleine's interrogation, and how Sarah and Mathieu had a baby daughter that she didn't know about.

"Sarah's not the killer," Clémence said. "There's a possibility, but I very much doubt it."

"Why didn't Mathieu tell you he had a baby?"

"I've been thinking about it. Maybe he would've told me before Charlotte barged in on us."

"Or maybe he purposely kept this from you," Arthur suggested. "I had the suspicion that he was trying to win you back. Didn't you think so?"

She thought about how Mathieu had looked at her that day in his room, questioning her about whether Arthur was right for her. When Charlotte showed up, she realized he'd only meant he was happy that his girlfriend understood his passion and wanted her to have the same.

She shook her head. "He has a girlfriend. Or had one. Why would he?"

"Because you're amazing. And you've been in the news lately. Maybe he wants your fame to rub off."

"No way." Although Mathieu had gotten a name for himself due to her status as an heiress and a socialite.

"And what was with the whole ghost thing?" Arthur said. "A baby handprint? It must've been his baby's handprint."

Clémence's eyes widened. Of course. The ghost incident had been pushed to the side, with all the murder stuff. "That's true. You're a genius. It was a very small handprint. It would make sense that it was his own baby's doing. The baby must've been over at his house."

"That's what's so strange. If Mathieu had a baby, wouldn't he come to the conclusion that it's his own baby's handprint? When you saw the handprint and noted how small it was, the topic of babies would've at least come up. He should've told you."

"Unless he doesn't know that he has a baby." She thought about what Sarah had said earlier. "But according to Sarah, he's paying child support, and he's promising her a bigger apartment and a nanny and all that. He must've known. Unless Sarah is crazy and delusional."

"One of them is lying." He cocked his head at her. "Do you think it's Sarah?"

Clémence thought about it. Sarah had no reason to lie—unless she was trying to elicit the sympathy of a well-connected socialite. But Sarah didn't seem interested in the scene. She didn't like modeling and being in the spotlight, and she seemed more keen on a normal life in Ireland. If she'd wanted to use Madeleine for her connections, she would've done so by now, instead of happily working at a perfume counter.

"No," she answered. "But why would Mathieu lie to me about the ghost?"

"He wants to get your attention. Maybe it was an excuse to get you to his place. He knows we're living together. Everybody knows that. I saw the way he was trying to worm his way into your apartment that night, trying to impress you with his interest in your painting."

Clémence shook her head. "Okay. Let's not talk about that. Let's focus on the case. Let's say Sarah's innocent. Who would want to kill Charlotte? Who has the most to gain from her death?"

"I don't know. This girl has connections to the art world. What exactly has she been doing for Mathieu? You know, if Mathieu didn't have an alibi, I would think he was responsible."

"That's what the inspector thought," Clémence said. "But like I said, he had an airtight alibi.

Besides, what would he have to gain by killing his own girlfriend?"

"Mathieu sounds more secretive than he lets on. Suppose Charlotte threatened to reveal something big? After all, he was keeping the baby a secret from you. Maybe she was going to tell you about the baby when he wanted to win you back. You did say that Charlotte was angry when you saw her. And she gets murdered on the same night?"

"I can't imagine what else Mathieu has to hide from me besides the whole baby thing."

"Clémence, you've said it yourself a million times: you never know who you can trust. You put Mathieu on a pedestal. He might not be the guy you think he is."

"I don't put him on a pedestal. I just think he's a talented artist, not some criminal or murderer."

"Well, Hitler was a talented artist, too. Food for thought."

"But we're wasting our time talking about Mathieu. Like I said, he has an alibi."

"Fine, but I still think there's something suspicious about him. He's probably hiding more than you think."

"I've known him for years, way longer than I've known you." She regretted it as soon as she said it, but it was too late to take it back now. "I just don't think he's involved in this. He's a nice guy."

"Nice?" he scoffed. "He cheated on you and kicked you out of your shared apartment."

"I chose to leave. Look, let's not do this. You're accusing someone based on your...personal conflicts."

You're jealous, she almost said, but she bit her tongue. He wasn't being a lot of help.

Except he was right about one thing: Charlotte's death could be connected to someone in the art world. Tomorrow, she'd have to continue with the investigation at the Madison gallery.

Chapter 13

The Madison Gallery was a modern art gallery located in the 6th arrondissement. While the neighboring galleries were full of tasteful black-and-white photography and scenic landscape paintings, the art at Madison was more experimental. It had an edge, while still remaining palatable for French buyers.

With exposed plumbing and white walls, the gallery space took up the street level floor of a Haussman building. Across the street was a Monoprix, and the gallery was sandwiched between an ice cream shop and an upscale toy store.

Clémence let herself in. There was no one else in sight. She was alone with the art. The oil paintings on the walls were by a Chinese artist named Liu Weng, who painted himself grinning and doing the thumbs-up in catastrophic world situations. Tiananmen Square. Hitler's inauguration speech. Third world starvation. His pieces were irreverent and controversial. A black blob-shaped statue sat in the middle of the gallery. It was simply titled "Disease."

Clémence could see Mathieu's new work fitting in at a gallery like this.

The place was pin-drop silent. Clémence had wanted to speak to the owner. According to her research, his name was Chris Kassabian. Charlotte had been his right-hand woman. Perhaps things were quiet because Charlotte wasn't in.

She waited, walking around, looking at the paintings, at Liu Weng's ridiculous grin.

"Exuberant, isn't it?" A male voice made her turn. He came out of a back room and approached her, his shoes clacking on the linoleum floor.

In a crisp white shirt and gray dress pants, Chris Kassabian was someone you'd pass on the street without a second glance. In his early sixties, he was almost as short as Clémence's five-foot-four frame. The most striking thing about the man was the way his eyes crinkled when he smiled.

"It's certainly unlike anything I've seen so far," Clémence said.

"Weng really pushes the envelope. He criticizes his own government, but he's extremely respected in China, to the goverment's chagrin. We're lucky to show him here. This series is the first that features him in the paintings."

"I suppose they can be self-portraits," Clémence said. "They're great. Funny social commentary."

"Have you heard of Weng?"

"No, I haven't. My parents are art collectors, though. They'd be interested if the paintings weren't so big."

Each painting was six feet tall. It would take up an entire wall of their apartment if she brought one home.

He chuckled. "You would definitely need to commit to his paintings. I'm Chris Kassabian, the owner."

"*Je suis* Clémence. *Enchantée.* I actually stopped by because a friend told me she worked here. Charlotte Lagrange? I thought I'd drop in and say hi."

His face fell at the mention of her. "Oh. Dear. Well—you haven't heard?"

"Heard what?" She blinked innocently.

"Charlotte is...She passed away."

Clémence gasped. She wouldn't be winning a César Award for Best Actress anytime soon, but Chris seemed to be buying it. "What? But how?"

"Well...were you a close friend?"

"I met her at a party just last week. We're more like acquaintances, but this is a complete shock!"

"All I know is that Charlotte was shot in her own apartment a couple of nights ago."

"*Mon dieu! Mais pourquoi?*" Why?

"I have no idea. She came from a respectable family, she was at the top of her class, and she was great as an employee."

"It's so bizarre. There are no leads?"

"Not as far as I know. I spoke to her parents, and they're in shock, too. Charlotte was a bright girl. She knew so much about art. All our clients loved her. I've been scrambling to find a replacement, but the girl was really something. She knew her stuff, and she could probably sell a framed napkin."

"So you don't know whether she had any enemies?" Clémence asked. "Maybe someone who was jealous of her?"

"No. I don't know much about her personal life, but I know she had a new boyfriend. I don't know much about him, though."

"Do you know whether she got along with her boyfriend?"

"As far as I could tell, she did. She was even trying to help him get a show here. His name was Mathieu something. He sounded promising, and I was considering his work, although we're booked until the end of the year. I haven't met him, however." He looked pensive for a moment. "It's rather depressing, isn't it? You work with someone for three years, and you realize you don't know them as well as you thought you did. I only know her through this job, her take on art. I know very little else about her."

"Hmm." Clémence nodded. "I wish I had gotten to know her better as well. She seemed so sharp. What were her opinions about art?"

"She was incredibly into modern art, discovering the best new artists. I felt like she was five years ahead. In the last couple of weeks, however, I was a little surprised to find that she was completely enraptured by a nineteenth century French painter."

"Who?"

"Felix Mercier, a painter from Normandy. Have you heard of him?"

Clémence tried to disguise her surprise. "No, I don't believe I have," she lied.

"Mercier wasn't as famous as his contemporaries, but, boy, was he good at painting light. Sunlight, moonlight, starlight. Charlotte really picked my brain about him. She was so interested in Merciers that she went to the Christie's showroom on Monday. There's one Mercier painting in the catalog that peaked her interest. As a matter of fact, she was registered to go to the auction at Christie's later today."

"Really?"

"Yes. Sad. She requested the afternoon off just to attend. A shame she won't make it."

Clémence decided she had to go to the auction and take Charlotte's place. Didn't Mathieu's roommate own a Mercier? That couldn't have been a coincidence, right? But the connection eluded her.

Chapter 14

At three fifteen p.m., Clémence went to the 8th arrondissement where Christie's was located. She was on time for the nineteenth-century European painting auction.

She registered under Charlotte's name and received a paddle and a catalog. This was where Charlotte had wanted to be. Clémence didn't know what she was looking for, but she was open to receiving any kind of clue or information.

She took a seat near the back and waited until the other chairs were filled and for the auction to begin. The paddle was in her hand, and it was a thrilling thought that she could raise it once and go home with a master's painting and a six-figure dent in her bank account. The people around her were mostly older, distinguished, or well-dressed types with poker faces. When the paintings were brought out, one by one, their faces did not betray their enthusiasm. A raise of the paddle was enough to signify their desire.

Clémence sat through paintings of children holding kittens, nudes of curvaceous women lying around in the grass, and scenes from the Bible. A small Renoir portrait of a young boy fetched eighty-five thousand euros. That had been an exciting one, with two serious bidders in the end causing a frenzy. Finally an Italian gentleman in an eccentric pink suit and an electric blue pocket square staked his claim.

After two more paintings were sold, Clémence saw a man around her age slip in. He had dark hair, glasses, and was average height. In black pants and a white dress shirt with the sleeves rolled up, he looked absolutely ordinary, except something about him looked familiar to Clémence. Had she met him before? She was sure they'd never spoken, but she'd seen that face somewhere. He didn't have an auction paddle. Did he work at Christie's? She'd come to the auctions in the past with her mother and might have met him then.

She also could've met him at a party. He must've been from a wealthy family, judging by his Gucci loafers and the Rolex on his wrist. What else could explain why someone so young would be interested in bidding on paintings that would cost some people a lifetime's salary?

They brought out the Mercier painting, the one Charlotte must've been interested in. It was of a boat on water during sunset. She'd seen that painting before. Where had she seen it?

Then it hit her.

On Mathieu's wall.

Surely it couldn't be the same painting. Mathieu said Gilles's was the original. Could it be that Mercier had similar paintings of the same subject?

Clémence looked through the catalog and found the photograph of the painting so she could examine it in detail. The untitled Mercier oil on canvas was dated 1878. It featured the same dazzling quality of sunlight reflecting red, orange, and gold in the water, something Mercier was a master at. It was an exact replica.

"Let's start the bidding at five thousand euros," the auctioneer said. "Do we have five thousand? Yes. Six thousand?..."

As bidders raised their paddles, Clémence squinted at the real painting on the platform. If the painting at Christie's was real, the one in Mathieu's must've been fake.

"Eighteen thousand. Yes, eighteen thousand. Do we have nineteen thousand?..."

The bespectacled young man in the white shirt never raised his paddle, but she noticed a trace of a self-satisfied smile on his face as he scanned the room, looking at the bidders.

It had come down to a stylish woman in her sixties with a white bob and a gentleman of the same age in a navy suit, balancing a cane against one knee.

"Fifty thousand! We have fifty thousand. Anyone else? Going once—going twice—sold!"

Clémence leaned back in her chair as the gavel struck. Had Charlotte known about Gilles's painting? Had she been interested in Mercier because she had a suspicion that the one Gilles owned was a fake?

Perhaps Charlotte had been involved in art fraud somehow, and that was why she was killed. But how? And which painting was the fake? The one that was just sold for fifty thousand euros, or the one that was hanging casually on a wall in Les Lilas?

It was imperative that she found out which one was fake. If Gilles's painting turned out to be authentic, then Christie's had a problem on their hands.

She went outside and jumped into a cab. She had the urge to see Gilles's painting again, and to get a sample so she could test it. Mathieu was probably at home painting, but she called him to make sure he was there. He didn't pick up.

After Clémence reached the house and paid the cab driver, Mathieu called back.

"Ça va, Clémence?" The usual flirtatious tone was in his voice. "You called?"

"Hey, Mathieu, are you home?"

"I'm about to go into a meeting with the same gallery owner I met for dinner this week. I think we're close to striking a deal. What's up?"

"Oh, I just wanted to talk to you about something."

"I don't know when I'll be done. It might be a couple of hours. Where are you? Do you want to meet near the gallery, or perhaps you want to come over to my place?"

"Why don't you call me when you're done, and I'll let you know where I am?"

"Great. I gotta go."

"*Bonne chance,*" she said. *Good luck.*

She didn't tell him that she was in front of his house. Perhaps something Arthur had said had stuck. She couldn't trust Mathieu one hundred percent. He'd lied about the small things. Even if he hadn't killed Charlotte, why did she have the suspicion that he was involved in all this somehow?

Since she was here, she was going to go see that painting again, one way or another.

She opened the gate and went around to the back yard. The window was open, to let the heat out of the part of the house Mathieu was using as a studio. She only had to push the window open more to reach the lock of the door from the inside. Looking around to make sure there weren't any witnesses, she took a lawn chair from the yard. By the window, she stood on the chair and reached an arm through the window to unlock the door.

Then, with a twist of the knob, she was in.

Chapter 15

"Hello?" Clémence called out. "Mathieu? Gilles? Anybody home?"

Unless the baby ghost was around, she was alone. As she passed the studio, a canvas on one of the easels caught her eye. Mathieu must've started a new painting. He'd only done the background, shades of red, orange and gold that looked achingly familiar. Why was Mathieu working on a small landscape painting when he was supposed to be finishing his series of portraits? The style was different too. His brushstrokes were usually bold and precise, while these were softer and more diluted, giving it a dreamy quality.

In the kitchen, she took a small sandwich bag from the drawer and grabbed a cutting knife. Her plan was to go directly to the Mercier painting, scrape a teensy sample of it into the bag so she could test the authenticity of the painting.

She headed up the stairs, and that was when she saw it: the small framed photograph on the mantelpiece. She picked up the photo of the man stroking a tamed tiger. It was Gilles, his hair in a buzz cut. He had on the same glasses and had the same nondescript face as the man Clémence had noticed earlier at Christie's. He'd looked especially pleased when the Mercier had sold for such a high price.

Mathieu did say that Gilles was out of town. But she'd seen him in Paris earlier that day. Had Mathieu lied to her again?

Mercier paintings...Gilles...Charlotte...they were all connected, but what was Gilles's connection to Charlotte exactly? Did he kill her? If so, why?

She could look in Gilles's room for clues. She went upstairs and tried the door. It was locked. What could he be hiding in that room?

Clémence bent down to look closely at the lock. It wasn't something that could be picked easily. And from what she remembered from the outside, the opaque curtains of his window were completely drawn.

She called a cab to pick her up from the house to take her back into central Paris.

In the cab, something stirred in her head, a possible formation of an explanation. But Clémence needed more information.

She might just make it to her art class at the Spinoza Atelier. Not that she was there to paint, as much as she wanted to. She needed to catch her classmate, Amelie. Clémence didn't have her number, and Amelie could really help her.

On the second floor of the building, Clémence reached Room Five just as students were spilling out.

"Clémence," Albert exclaimed. "Look Rita, Clémence is back."

Albert and Rita were her classmates. In their sixties, they were an old married couple, both talented painters with different styles.

"We haven't seen you in so long," Rita said with a kind smile. "We heard you were kidnapped. Are you okay?"

"It was a bit of a bother," Clémence joked. "But I'm totally fine."

"We figured you needed a break to deal with everything," Rita said. "Will you be back for the next class?"

"Certainly. At least, if all goes well. Hey, was Amelie in class today? I need to talk to her."

"Yes, she's inside, packing."

Just then the girl in question came out carrying her tote bag of art supplies. At twenty, Amelie was studying art restoration and she was taking painting classes as a hobby. At the sight of Clémence, her green eyes lit up.

"Clémence, hey! I was wondering when you'd be back."

Like the others, Amelie also expressed surprise and concern about what she'd read about her in the news, but Clémence assured her, as she had with everyone, that all was well.

"Actually, I'm here to see you," Clémence said. "I need your help."

"My help?"

"You study art restoration, right?"

"Yes."

"I need to authenticate a painting, a valuable Mercier painting, to see whether it's real or a forgery. I have a picture of it and I've taken some paint samples." Clémence gave her the photograph and the sample in the Ziplock bag. "Do you know anybody from your program, perhaps a peer or a professor, who can run some tests?"

"I have a professor who's a renowned art expert, so sure, it's possible. We have the technology to do that. Have you found a Mercier that you think is a fake?"

"It's a friend's," Clémence said. "But it's actually quite urgent that I find out. When do you think you can do this?"

"I was just going to a class right now, actually. I'm sure I can ask my professor, if he's at his office today. Maybe we can start on it tomorrow."

"Great! I'll owe you big time, Amelie."

"It'll be my pleasure. It'll actually be a fun, hands-on learning experience. No problem."

Clémence beamed and gave Amelie a hug. "Thanks so much!"

Now that authenticating the painting was taken care of, Clémence had another person to visit: Sarah.

Chapter 16

The world-famous Galerie Lafayette department store sold everything from high-end clothing to home furnishings and gourmet food. The ten-story building's Bell Epoque architecture was dazzling, and the dramatic colored dome had all the tourists looking up and snapping pictures as soon as they stepped inside.

The perfume and cosmetics section, where Clémence would find Sarah, was on the ground floor. Clémence spotted her at the Marcus Savin perfume counter, smiling and talking to two customers. Sarah's cheeks were plumper due to her slight weight gain, but Clémence didn't think the remnants of her pregnancy weight made her any less beautiful. For so long, Clémence had hated her while finding her intimidatingly gorgeous, but now Sarah seemed to be radiant. Perhaps it was because she had become a mother.

As Clémence approached her, she felt shy. She'd prepared what she was going to say, but speaking to Sarah would still be awkward.

At the counter, Clémence pretended to look at the beautiful glass bottles of Marcus Savin's perfumes. Clémence knew the designer, and didn't realize that his perfumes were so popular that they warranted their own stall in Galerie Lafayette. When Sarah finished ringing up a customer's order, she turned her attention to Clémence.

Clémence faked surprise. "Sarah?"

"Yes." Sarah blinked at her before recognition lit her eyes. "Oh, Clémence? Hi."

"Hi."

Sarah gave her a shy smile, then told her she'd been reading a lot about her. Clémence answered the usual kidnapping questions and made small talk.

"I love these perfumes," she said. Marcus had sent her some of his clothes and three bottles of his perfumes last week as a gift, so Clémence wasn't lying.

"So do I," Sarah replied.

"Oh. Is that why you're working here?" Clémence hoped she didn't sound patronizing because she wasn't trying to be. Sarah only smiled again sweetly, and didn't seem to take it the wrong way.

"Honestly, I'm working here because I need the money." Sarah laughed.

Clémence felt more at ease with Sarah being so frank with her. "Growing up, I always thought it would be fun to work here."

"It can be. You get to meet a lot of interesting people. And there's the discounts."

"Discounts are always good," Clémence said. "I heard you had a baby, so congratulations."

"Thanks." She flashed her pearly white teeth once again. "Who told you? Mathieu?"

"Yes," Clémence lied.

"I thought Mathieu didn't want people to know, but I suppose you're not just anyone. He told me he got in touch with you again."

"It's been fun to catch up. All that stuff's in the past, so why not be friends?"

"Exactly," Sarah said. "That's my attitude."

"But why doesn't Mathieu want people to know he has a daughter?"

"He says wants to establish himself as a young painter. I don't know why exactly, but he says it's important for his career. And it's not as if anybody's writing about us these days, anyway, so it doesn't matter."

"Did his girlfriend know?"

"He has a girlfriend?" Sarah asked.

Her face was unreadable. "Oh, you didn't know?"

"No. I know he dates sometimes, but he never told me about a girlfriend."

"Well, Sarah," Clémence said. "I'm glad I ran into you because there are some things I want to tell you. Mathieu's girlfriend was an art gallery assistant named Charlotte Lagrange and she was killed recently. Shot in the head."

Clémence gave her the full story and told her about how Charlotte had been keen on Mercier paintings, while Gilles owned one. "I think Mathieu's roommate is connected to her murder somehow. What do you know about him?"

"Gilles?" Sarah's expression soured. "I've only met him a few times. To tell you the truth, he gives me the creeps, the way he leers at me. You don't think he killed this girl, do you?"

"I don't know. I'm trying to figure it out. What can you tell me about him?"

"Mathieu moved in with him about three months ago. I don't know how he met Gilles exactly. Mathieu mentioned something about meeting him at a party."

"Have you been over to Mathieu's house a lot since he moved there?"

Sarah shook her head. "Just when I'm dropping Joy—she's our baby—at his house on Saturdays, when he gets her all day. He doesn't really want to let me see the place. He says it's because he's working on some new paintings and doesn't want anyone to see them."

"So he's able to take care of the baby by himself?"

"Sure. Mathieu's a good father. I'm iffy about the baby being around this roommate, though. Something about him is just so slick."

"He's out of town at the moment, isn't he?" Clémence asked. "For the whole month?"

"Not as far as I know. When I dropped off Joy last Saturday, I saw him. He didn't see me, though, because I left before he could spot me and start leering."

"Oh, that's funny. I thought Gilles was in London." At *least that's what Mathieu claims*, Clémence thought.

"I wish he was in London, so he'd stop coming in here to flirt with me."

"He does that?" Clémence asked.

"Sometimes. Whenever he's in the neighborhood."

"When was he here last?"

"Two days ago. Just hanging around the stall, asking me questions about perfumes and not buying anything."

Gilles was definitely in town. The question was, why was Mathieu trying to hide him from her?

Chapter 17

Galerie Lafayette's rooftop terrace was the place to be to enjoy an ice cream and pass the afternoon with friends. As the sunny weather streak was still going strong, locals and tourists had the same idea. Clémence bought a chocolate cone and waited for Mathieu to show up. She took in the sweeping view of the city. The back of the Opera Garnier could be seen, as well as Clémence's good friend, *la Tour Eiffel*, hanging back in the distance.

You could call Paris a lot of things, but you couldn't call it ugly, she thought. It was a shame that the people had to ruin a place of beauty by committing heinous crimes.

When Mathieu showed up, she'd long since finished her cone. He was beaming. Should he be looking this happy only days after his girlfriend's death? Perhaps he'd forgotten that he was supposed to be in mourning.

After he greeted her with *bisous* that lingered seductively close to her mouth, Clémence said, "Hey, it's funny. I ran into Sarah downstairs. I didn't know she worked here."

"Oh, Sarah. Right. She does. You met her?" He looked concerned.

"She helped me with some perfumes. But I didn't end up buying anything. We did have a chat, though."

His smile faltered. "You didn't talk about me, did you?"

"What's there to talk about?" she joked.

He laughed in response. He looked relieved. Too relieved. "Phew. Two ex-girlfriends coming together—that could've been lethal."

"What's the news with your gallery?"

"They're going to reach a decision by tomorrow," he said. "Fingers crossed. There's a pretty good chance they'll show my work. They're a great gallery. It'll certainly boost my reputation."

"I'm sure you'll get it," Clémence said. "You're good at what you do."

"Thanks, Clémence. You've been so supportive during this tough time." He stepped in closer, mesmerizing her with his light blue eyes. "You know, I've really missed you. You're the only person who understands me. I made a grave mistake being with Sarah, and I wish I could turn back time."

Clémence tried to maintain the smile on her face. *Sarah is the mother of your baby*, she wanted to snap. *Have you forgotten that you have a baby?*

"I really think we make a good team," Mathieu continued. "I know you're with Mr. PhD and you like him. He's all right, I guess, but he's a little boring for you, don't you think?"

"Arthur is—"

"I still have feelings for you," Mathieu blurted. "If you feel the same way, life is too short. What I took away from Charlotte's death is this: if you want something in life, grab it, and I definitely want you, Clémence Damour."

He leaned in to kiss her. Clémence turned her cheek, and he kissed her there instead. "I'm flattered, Mathieu. But you know that—"

"I know, I know. Your boyfriend, Arthur." He stepped back to give her space. "Just think about it, Clémence. We're meant to be together. We can be one of those great artist couples, like Frida Kahlo and Diego Rivera."

"But they were miserable. They cheated on each other."

"You know what I mean. We have a lot to learn from each other. And you're so adventurous. You proved that when you went around the world. I'd always thought you didn't like living life on the edge. You're so different now, like you're a new woman. Maybe we needed to be apart for a while so we can find ourselves before finding each other again."

"Mathieu..."

"Okay, I'll stop talking about it. You know where I stand now, and I'll leave it up to you to decide."

"Thanks."

They were silent for a moment, looking out at the cityscape.

"How's your roommate?" Clémence brought up casually. "Is he still in London?"

"Yeah. He just called yesterday. Said he'd be back this weekend. I'm glad he'll be around again. You know, with this whole ghost situation. Yesterday I really wasn't able to sleep, because I kept hearing noises."

"The ghost's been keeping you awake?" Clémence tried not to let any sarcasm creep into your voice.

"Maybe you want to come over one night," he said flirtatiously. "We'll film it and make *Paranormal Activity* 9."

"Maybe." Clémence met his gaze, smiling in what she hoped was a seductive way. "I better be going. Arthur is going to be coming home soon, and there's something I want to talk to him about. You know, about our relationship. Something between us hasn't been right for some time."

Mathieu nodded sympathetically. "Do what you have to do."

They gave each other *bisous* good-bye, and Clémence promised she'd call soon.

When she exited Galerie Lafayette onto Boulevard Haussman, Amelie called her.

"Hey Clémence," Amelie said. "We ran some tests this morning on the Mercier painting. It turned out that one of the pigments used wasn't invented until 1934. Since the painting is dated 1878, the painting is a fake. From what I can tell from the photograph, it's a pretty good forgery."

Clémence had suspected this all along. But what about the one from the auction? Did somebody pay fifty thousand euros for a fake Mercier?

Chapter 18

The next day, Clémence wore a little black dress, courtesy of Marcus Savin, and red leather pumps. She was looking her best as she rang Mathieu's door in the late evening.

She'd come uninvited, and she heard voices from outside the door. Gilles was home.

When she rang the doorbell again, Mathieu opened the door and received her with surprise.

"Clémence. I didn't know you were coming by. It's nice to see you." He gave her a once-over. "You look drop-dead sexy."

"Thanks," Clémence said breezily, stepping into the house as if she owned the place. "So it's settled. I talked to Arthur, and now I'm here to talk to you."

She plopped down on the cream leather couch, and he sat down next to her, looking at her at with puppy eyes. "What is it?"

"I told Arthur everything. He was very understanding about the whole situation."

Mathieu couldn't help but smirk. "Hope he wasn't too hurt."

"No." Clémence smirked back. "Actually, he was very relieved."

"How come?"

Clémence turned to the staircase. "Hey, I heard voices before I came in. Is your roommate back?"

"Oh," he said slowly, as if he was unsure of answering. "Yeah. He's back."

"I'd like to meet him," Clémence said.

"Sure, I'll get him."

Mathieu disappeared upstairs, and came down a minute later with the bespectacled man Clémence had recognized at Christie's. He was growing in a light beard that day, and he wore a blue dress shirt with the sleeves rolled up.

"This is Clémence," Mathieu said. "Clémence, Gilles."

"A pleasure to meet you." Gilles spoke in French with a British accent.

She could see why Sarah would be creeped out by him. His dark eyes seemed to devour every curve of her body.

"Nice to finally meet you," Clémence said. "Did you enjoy your trip to London?"

"Very much so. It was a mixture of business and pleasure, since I got to see some friends."

"Did any portion of the trip involve murder?" Clémence asked nonchalantly.

Both men gaped at her in shock.

"Excuse me?" Gilles demanded.

"You heard me." Clémence's voice turned dead serious. "Charlotte Lagrange, Mathieu's girlfriend. You killed her, didn't you?"

Gilles sputtered, then broke out into a laugh. "Why would I kill her?"

"Because she was getting in the way," Clémence said. "She was going to expose your art fraud scheme. Your reputation would've been ruined. You'd lose millions and you'd go to jail."

"That's ridiculous."

"Mathieu said you were in London, but you've been spotted around Paris. Weren't you at Christie's, making sure your fake Mercier sold for a good price?"

"Clémence," Mathieu cut in. "You don't know you what you're talking about."

"Can it, Mathieu," Clémence said, anger rising in her voice. "Don't think I don't know your part in all this. Why did you tell me that Gilles wasn't in town? So you could try to seduce me in this house. Isn't that also why you didn't tell me you already have a baby with Sarah? That wouldn't have fit in with your plan to win me back so you can use me for my fame and make a name for yourself in the art world again. You used me once, and you won't use me again."

"Really, Clémence, that's preposterous. Do you know how ridiculous that sounds?"

"Is it? Isn't that why Charlotte died? She was an inconvenience for the both of you. She was onto you, Mathieu, and she got jealous once she figured out that you were trying to win me back. She knew that you were done with her and her limited connections in the art world. Besides, you already got what you wanted from her: a recommendation to a reputable gallery. That night after I left, she must've let you know that she was onto your plan to make Mercier copies for Gilles to sell. And copies of other great lost paintings. She threatened you. You told Gilles, and he must've made the snap decision to kill her on the spot. You guys didn't expect anyone to trace this back to you, did you?"

Mathieu's lips were were pressed in a grimace. "Clémence." His tone dropped two octaves.

"Showing up at my house the night Gilles murdered her was a good touch," Clémence said, "so I wouldn't suspect you. And to feel sorry for you so you could get closer to me. At least that was a bit smarter than your original plan—using your baby to make the handprint, then baiting me to come here on some lame ghost story."

"You believed it, didn't you?" Mathieu said.

"You're so pathetic," Clémence spat. "Did you really expect me to dump my amazing boyfriend for a con artist like you? What happened to you? You could've made it on talent alone. Why did you do it?"

"Get off your high horse, Clémence." Mathieu snapped. His face twisted into fury. "It's people like you who I hate. Everything always comes so easy for you. If you wanted your own exhibit, I'm sure you'd get anything you want with a snap of your fingers, with your name alone, and talent would mean squat. Me? I have no name; I have no wealth. I graduated and expected the world to recognize my talent like everyone did in school, but you know what? They're all idiots. As you said, my work is ahead of my time. I refuse to be a slave to everyone's ignorance and mediocrity. So I did what I had to do to live comfortably. When Gilles approached me to make copies of famous masters to pass off as the real things, I didn't have to think twice." He let out a bitter laugh. "People are so stupid. They bought it. And my first Mercier easily passed for the real thing at one of the most prestigious auction houses in the world. It was easier than I thought."

"And Charlotte?" Clémence demanded. "You have no remorse that your so-called business partner killed her?"

Mathieu shrugged. "It's her own fault. Things were going well, and we could've had fun for a couple of months—that is, until she decided to stick her nose in our business."

"How did you know about the fakes?" Gilles asked. His was looking at her with burning hatred. "How could you have possibly found out?"

"I was here yesterday," Clémence said.

Gilles and Mathieu looked at each other. "You were?" Mathieu said.

"Yup. I wanted to get in to take a closer look at your Mercier, but you were out, so I let myself in."

"What?" Gilles's mouth hung open.

"I saw the new painting that Mathieu was working on. I realized later that you were making a copy of another Mercier painting, of the sunset over the field of lavender in Provence. It's a pretty good deal for you, huh, Mathieu? You have all the space to work on your own paintings, while you rip off respectable collectors."

"Do you blame me?" Mathieu spat. "It was the only way to make it. I didn't want to be a starving artist. Screw that entire ideology. Artists had to suffer for centuries due to the general public's idiocy. Those people wouldn't know art if it bit them in the ass. Real or fake, they'll buy whatever so-called experts tell them is worthy of being owned."

"You made your daughter proud," Clémence shook her head.

"You know what, Clémence? You're the pathetic one. You were always pathetic, following me around like a lost puppy. Where's your great artistic achievement, huh? You're just jealous, like you always were."

Clémence took a deep breath. "You know, I used to have respect for you. But what's the point of being talented when you're unscrupulous and have no morals? Art is about revealing the soul. Is that why your new paintings are so dark and disturbing? But it doesn't matter, does it? Your career is over. Murder and art fraud—you're finished."

"Shut up," Gilles said coldly. "You've spoken for long enough. Now if you know all this, why would you come to the house of a murderer?"

Clémence gave him a strange look. "Who said I came alone?"

On cue, the police burst in through the front door.

"Freeze! You're under arrest."

Inspector Cyril St. Clair entered, after several armed policeman. He watched with delight as the men were handcuffed.

"Bravo, boys," Clémence said. "Your confession has been recorded. That'll make the trial a lot faster."

Clémence pulled down the collar of her black dress to reveal a hidden mic taped to her chest.

Arthur also entered, smiling smugly. He stared Mathieu down, who looked away in disgust. Arthur hugged Clémence. "You were amazing."

Clémence turned back Mathieu and Gilles. "You didn't think I'd be stupid enough to come without backup, did you? When your Mercier turned out to be a fake, I went to the police with my suspicions that you were making copies in this house. They also ran a test on the Mercier that had been sold at the auction. Surprise, surprise—that turned out to be a fake, too. The police backed my theory, and I came here and got your confessions. I'm sure that there is more evidence in Gilles's room that the police would love to get their hands on. I wouldn't be surprised if there were more fakes in there."

"We also found a footprint at the murder scene," Cyril added, not to be outdone. "I'm sure we'll find a matching shoe, Gilles. You're going away for a long time, boys."

Clémence turned to Mathieu. "What do you want to tell your daughter?"

His pale eyes were blank. "Nothing. Tell her nothing."

Chapter 19

The night before Clémence's birthday, she wore a slinky black dress and stepped out on the balcony of her apartment. The moon was an oversized orange, perched above the rooftop of a neighboring building. The Eiffel Tower stood high and mighty across the Seine. In less than ten minutes, it would shimmer, as it did every hour on the hour after sundown.

A red tablecloth covered the balcony table. A single candle was placed on top. Arthur had set it with the meal that he'd cooked—pasta, as that was the only thing he *could* cook, but she was pleased nonetheless. He'd made an effort to learn to make something more complicated from his family chef: smoked salmon, mushrooms, and sun-dried tomatoes were thrown into the mix, with a light creamy sauce.

When she came out, he was pouring champagne into their flutes.

"You look beautiful tonight," he said as she took her seat.

"Just tonight?" she teased.

"Every night. You look beautiful twenty-four, seven."

"That's better." She placed the napkin on her lap.

When she tried his pasta, she smiled in delight. "This is actually pretty good."

"You sound surprised," Arthur said.

"Does this mean you're going to cook for me all the time?"

He laughed. "Let's just start with special occasions for now. Becoming your slave is a gradual process."

"Maybe I'll hire you to cook at Damour," she said.

"Happy birthday." He gazed deep into her eyes. "Je t'aime."

Clémence's birthday party was tomorrow, and she was closing down Damour for the evening to have it. She realized that birthdays weren't just about getting older, but to celebrate her life and the people she loved and got to share it with. She had to make the most of the good in her life, and there was plenty of good.

At almost twenty-nine, she'd surrounded herself with people she could trust. Through trial and error, she'd shed her naïveté and learned to be more discerning. She'd especially grown in the past few months when she'd faced more of the darkness of humanity than she'd ever experienced before in her life.

As she expressed all this to Arthur, he took her hand and kissed it.

"But I hope you maintain some of your innocence and curiosity," he said. "Even if it gets you in trouble sometimes."

"Only if you don't scold me when I do."

"I have to admit, I did think there was a chance that I'd lose you to Mathieu," he admitted.

"Really? Honesty is important to me. Mathieu broke my trust, and there was no way I would've forgiven him. I was only interested and making amends and being friends, that was all. Now, unfortunately, it's beyond repair."

Sarah had been devastated when Madeleine and Clémence paid her a visit to break the news. She planned on moving back to Ireland, since Mathieu was not the kind of father figure she wanted for her daughter.

"I thought there was some unfinished business there," Arthur said. "He was your first big love. I'd never really been in love before you, so I didn't know what to think."

Clémence took in his adorable face. Arthur could really surprise her sometimes with just how sweet and romantic he was. "Well, stop worrying, because I'd never been as in love with anyone as I have with you, either. Hopefully things will simmer down, and we can enjoy the rest of the summer in peace."

Arthur chuckled. "I doubt that. Now that your ex has been arrested, the paparazzi are not going to loosen up anytime soon."

Clémence sighed. "I wish I could take a vacation."

"You know, that's not a bad idea. I'm submitting my PhD tomorrow. Just before your party."

"Really?" Clémence exclaimed. "You're done? You never told me that!"

He nodded proudly. "That's why I've been so busy recently. J&D offered me a full-time contract, but I don't need to start immediately. Why don't we go away?"

"Where do you want to go?" Clémence asked.

"I have that place in Honfleur," Arthur said, referring to the house that his family owned. "It's empty, so we'll have the place to ourselves. All the Parisians are in the south of France in the summer, so the beaches there won't be too crowded."

"So let's go. Just the two of us."

Clémence finished the rest of her pasta, thinking it was the best thing she'd ever tasted because it was made with love by the man she loved.

Recipes

Okay, so making croissants is a bit of a process, but it's worth it. It might seem confusing at first, but follow the steps, and you'll end up with croissants that resemble something you'd find in your local bakery. And if they don't, I'm sure they'll taste good anyway!

Recipe #1

Classic French Croissant

Makes 16

For dough
- 4 cups all purpose flour
- 1/2 cup + 2 tbsp. cold whole milk
- 1/4 cup + 2 tbsp. granulated sugar
- 1/2 cups + 2 tbsp. cold water
- 3 tbsp. soft unsalted butter
- 1 tbsp. + 1/2 tsp. instant yeast
- 2 1/4 tsp. table salt

For butter layer
- 1 1/4 cups cold unsalted butter

For egg wash
- 1 large egg

For the dough

Combine dough ingredients in a mixing bowl and mix on low speed for 3 minutes, scraping sides of bowl once if needed. Mix for 3 minutes on medium speed. Transfer dough to a lightly floured 10-inch pie pan or a dinner plate. Flour top of dough lightly. Wrap well in plastic to prevent it from drying and refrigerate overnight.

Make the butter layer: On day 2, cut cold butter lengthwise into half-inch slabs. Place slabs to form a 5 or 6 inches square on a piece of parchment paper. Place another piece of parchment paper on top. Use a rolling pin to pound out butter until it's about 7.5 inches square. Put in the fridge as you roll out the dough.

Laminate dough: On a lightly floured work surface, unwrap dough. Roll into a square measuring 10 to 12 inches. Take the butter out from the fridge. It should be cold but pliable.

Place butter on top of dough to form a diamond atop the square beneath. The points of the butter square should be centered along the sides of the dough so the flaps of the dough can be folded over the butter. Fold all four flaps of the dough to the center of the butter so it resembles a square envelope. Press edges together to completely seal the butter in the dough. This way, the butter won't escape.

Lightly flour top and bottom of dough. Use rolling pin to firmly press on the dough to elongate it slightly. Roll, focusing on lengthening rather than widening. Keep edges straight. Roll until it's about 8 x 24 inches. Keep square shape; reshape corners with hands if needed. Brush flour off dough.

Fold dough into thirds, like the way you would fold a letter. Put dough on a baking sheet, cover with plastic wrap, and freeze for 20 minutes.

Take out and repeat the rolling process. Roll dough until it's back to 8 x 24 inches. Fold in thirds again. Brush off excess flour. Cover and freeze for another 20 minutes.

Take out and repeat rolling and folding process. Put dough on baking sheet and cover with plastic. Tuck plastic under all four sides and refrigerate overnight.

Divide dough: On day 3, unwrap and lightly flour top and bottom of dough. Lengthen dough with rolling pin. Roll dough into a narrow strip, 8 x 44 inches. If dough is sticky, sprinkle with flour. (If it resists rolling and shrinks back before you get there, fold dough back into thirds, cover, and refrigerate for 10 minutes.)

Lift the dough an inch or so off the table at its midpoint and allow it to shrink from both sides. This helps prevent the dough from shrinking when it's cut. Make sure there's extra dough on either side to allow you to trim ends so they're straight. Trim.

Lay a yardstick or a tape measure lengthwise along top of dough. Use a knife to mark dough at 5-inch intervals (7 marks in total) on one side. On the other side, make the first mark, 2.5 inches in from one end, then make 5-inch intervals starting from that point. You'll have 8 marks that hallway between the marks of the opposite side.

With a pizza wheel or a knife, and a yardstick to guide you, cut the dough diagonally from top mark to bottom mark, changing the angles to make triangles. You'll end up with 15 triangles, plus a small scrap of dough at each end.

Shape croissants: Lay triangle on a workspace with the fatter end closest to you. Roll dough away from you. Roll dough all the way down its length until the pointed end of the triangle is directly underneath the croissant. Bend the two legs toward you to form the crescent shape. Gently press tips of legs together to help keep this shape. (They won't stay touching).

Shape remaining croissants the same way.

Proof croissants: Whisk egg with 1 tsp water in a small bowl until smooth to make the egg wash. Lightly brush it on each croissant.

Refrigerate remaining egg wash, as you'll need it again. Wherever you proof your croissants, make sure temperature is not so warm that the butter melts out of dough. Preferably a draft-free spot at 75 to 80°F.

Bake Croissants: Brush croissants with egg wash for a second time before putting them into a 425°F oven. After 10 minutes, rotate sheets. If baking two sheets at the time, also swap their positions in the oven. Continue baking until bottoms are an even brown and the tops are richly browned, with the edges showing signs of coloring (about 8 to 10 more minutes). If they darken too quickly, lower oven temperature by 10°F.

Let cool on racks. They're best served warm. If not, they can be reheated and eaten within 1 to 2 days.

Tip: Add flavor to your croissants by using the ingredient of your choice. Nutella, jam, chocolate, ham and cheese can all be rolled up within the croissant dough.

Recipe # 2

Pain au Chocolat

*M*ade from the same layered dough as croissants, the *pain au chocolat* (chocolate bread) is golden and crispy on the outside and melted chocolate swirled around the inside. They're also known as "chocolatine" or chocolate croissant.

Makes 12
- 3 1/2 cups bread flour
- 1/2 cup milk
- 1/2 cup lukewarm water
- 4 tsp instant dried yeast
- 1/3 cup granulated sugar
- 1 cup butter, softened
- 3 tbsp butter, melted and cooled
- 9 ounces bittersweet or semisweet chocolate, coarsely chopped
- 1 egg
- 2 tbsp milk
- 1 1/2 tsp salt

Dissolve yeast in lukewarm water for 5 minutes. Add flour, sugar, milk, melted butter, and salt; and mix the dough on medium speed for 2 minutes. If dough is too sticky, add 1 tablespoon of extra flour at a time until dough is firm enough to hold a shape.

Shape dough into a ball and loosely cover with plastic wrap. Rest at room temperature for 30 minutes. Roll dough into a 10-inch by 15-inch rectangle. Cover loosely and let rise for 40 minutes.

Brush dough with softened butter. Fold dough into thirds, like a letter. Roll dough back into a 10-inch x 15-inch rectangle shape. Fold dough into thirds again and cover with plastic wrap. Put in fridge for 1 hour. Repeat this process one more time.

Cut dough into 12 rectangles with a sharp knife. Arrange a line of chopped chocolate along one end of rectangle. Roll it once. Press down lightly. Roll it again. Add another line of chocolate. Roll and press down again. Keep rolling. Keep ends under the pastry.

Arrange finished *pain au chocolat* on a lightly greased baking sheet. Leave at least 1.5 inches between each pastry. Cover loosely with plastic wrap. Let rise for 45 minutes to 1 hour until doubled in size.

Preheat oven to 400F. Whisk egg and 2 table-spoons of milk together to make an egg wash.

Brush egg wash across the surface of each pastry. Bake for 12 to 14 minutes, until puffy and golden brown.

Recipe #3

Croissant aux Amandes

*H*ere is an easy and delicious recipe for almond croissants using leftover buttered croissants.

Makes 8

- 8 croissants, day old and left at room temperature overnight
- 1 cup water
- 1/2 cup granulated sugar
- 1 cup almond meal/almond flour
- 1/8 tsp salt
- 1 stick (8 tbsp) unsalted butter, room temperature and sliced
- 2 large eggs
- 3 tbsp sliced almonds
- 2 tbsp sugar
- 4 tbsp rum or 1 tsp vanilla extract (optional)
- Powdered sugar for dusting

For the syrup

Combine 1 cup water, 2 tbsp sugar, and 4 tbsp rum in a small saucepan. Bring to simmer for 1 minute, and stir until the sugar dissolves. Remove from heat and let cool.

For the almond filling: In the bowl of a stand mixer fitted with the paddle attachment, combine 1 cup almond meal, 1/2 cup granulated sugar, and 1/8 tsp salt. Mix until well incorporated, then blend in the butter. Add eggs one at a time until mixture is creamy and fluffy.

Assembling the almond croissant: Preheat oven to 350F. Line a cookie sheet with parchment paper. Slice day-old croissants in half, like you would for a sandwich. Dip croissants one by one into syrup, coating both sides and ends well. They should be moist but not soaking wet.

Arrange croissants on sheet with cut side up. Spread about 2 tbsp of almond filling on it, and place other croissant half on top. Spread about 1 tbsp of almond filling on top, and sprinkle with sliced almonds.

Bake on center rack for 15 to 18 minutes, or until the cream is golden. Transfer to rack to cool. Can be eaten warm. Dust with powdered sugar before serving.

Recipe #4

Apple Pie Croissant

Makes 16

- French croissant dough
- 1 apple
- 1/2 tsp sugar
- 1/2 tsp brown sugar
- 1/2 tsp ground cinnamon
- 1/2 tsp pumpkin pie spice or 1/2 tsp apple pie spice

Preheat oven to 375°F. Peel, core, and chop apple. Combine apple, sugars, cinnamon, and pie spice. Lightly sauté over low heat.

See Recipe #1 on how to roll and cut dough. Cut into 16 triangles. Divide up apple mixture. Scoop mixture on dough and roll up as you would a regular croissant.

Bake on a sheet for 12–15 minutes, or until lightly browned.

About the Author

Harper Lin lives in Kingston, Ontario with her husband, daughter, and Pomeranian puppy. When she's not reading or writing mysteries, she's in yoga class, hiking, or hanging out with her family and friends. *The Patisserie Mysteries* draws from Harper's own experiences of living in Paris in her twenties. She is currently working on more cozy mysteries.

www.HarperLin.com

Made in the USA
Columbia, SC
20 June 2020